The Fire Starter

The Fire Starter

Jess Parker

For my Mum
Auntie Sa
And Chloé

Author: Jess Parker
Cover design: Chloé Moverley
ISBN: 9789403697581

Publisher: Bookmundo

Chapter 1

It was so weird to think that this was our new home. I couldn't imagine life without Dad in this crummy little flat. It just wasn't right. I sat alone on the floor of my new bedroom, surrounded by cardboard boxes, whilst the moving people lugged our furniture all the way up to the fifth floor. We'd been evicted from our old house when Dad left, and Mum couldn't afford to keep paying the bills. Her job as a cleaner didn't pay very well.

Andrea and Theo, my younger twin brother and sister, loved Dad more than anything. He would play princesses with Andrea and do silly high-pitched voices and he'd play football with Theo and always let him score goals. Because they were only three when he left Mum told them that he had just gone on holiday, and we would see him again soon. The youngest of the family, Clover, hadn't yet said her first word when Dad left, so his absence didn't particularly bother her. But being the oldest, I knew that Dad wasn't coming back.

"Ember!" called Mum from the front door. That's me. I'm Ember. Like the heart of a fire. That's what Dad used to tell me. I blinked, slightly surprised at suddenly being pulled away from my thoughts. I slowly rose to my feet, traipsed

down the hall and entered the new living room. "Thanks," Mum said to the delivery men before shutting the door.
"Yes Mum, what did you need?" I asked.
"Oh there you are! I wondered what you were up to. We're going to start unpacking now, just to get it over and done with. Your stuff has been put in your bedrooms already, so all you'll need to do is put your things where you want them. While you do that I'm gonna move the last of the furniture around a bit."
"Sure." I said. Andrea got up from the floor and skipped down the hall and Theo, much less enthusiastically, followed.

The twin's room was small, cramped and was probably meant to be a large storage cupboard but it would do. Their new bunk bed fitted, as did the chest of drawers and a desk. I looked down at the mountain of junk on the floor and sighed before saying "Come on then kids. Let's unpack." It took a while because Theo kept chucking his pants around the room and Andrea insisted upon making sure everything was absolutely perfect, but in the end everything was in its place. Once they'd finished I said "Okay, let's go and get you guys something to drink. It's been a long day."

I took them back out into the living room where Mum was giving baby Clover a snack. I eventually found two cups in a random box amongst all the mess, as well as a bottle of lemonade in a cool bag. The twins sat down on the sofa, guzzling lemonade, sharing a bag of crisps, and watching their favourite show on our old iPad. I wanted to sit down with them and relax but my new room had to be sorted out too.

I went back to my room and opened one of the many boxes and started putting all my belongings away. This was quickly accomplished and feeling like everything was ready, I went back out to sit with the twins.

Mum breathed a sigh of relief and sank into an armchair as I appeared in the doorway. She'd finished moving all the furniture around and had made this cramped and stuffy flat seem like home. Well, sort of. "All finished Mum?" I asked, flopping into the armchair opposite.
"Yep," Mum smiled. She'd clearly been very hard at work because she was pink in the face and shiny with sweat. "I've got everything running smoothly. The water, WIFI, and electricity. I've also put every last thing in its place, dusted and hoovered the whole flat, cleaned the bathroom and the kitchen and I'll be serving dinner in a few minutes."
"Wow Mum. That didn't take long. You must be exhausted. You're brilliant! I think you should have a well-deserved rest."
"No, that's alright. I need to look after you lot."
"We'll be fine! You'll only be in the next room. Plus, they're already in their Pj's. All there is to do is feed them and brush their teeth." I replied.
"Are you sure that's alright? Thanks Honey," She got up from the chair and sloped wearily off to her room.

There was a bing from the kitchen, and as there weren't any doors separating the living room from the kitchen-dining room, I could see it was the little egg timer that had made the sound. I turned off the oven and found a pair of oven gloves after opening practically every drawer there was, then took out the tray of fries and fish fingers before getting the sweetcorn out of the microwave. After finding plates and cutlery, I laid the table and called the kids over for tea. Theo and Andrea sat down and hoovered up their dinners. As the twins ate, I spoon-fed Clover a tub of pureed apples then put her to bed and sat Andrea and Theo in front of the TV with milk and cookies.

A little while later we went off to bed. I'd never normally go to bed at the same time as the twins, but it had been a long day and I found it hard to keep my eyes open. After brushing their teeth and reading them two quick bedtime stories, I curled up in bed. It took a long time for sleep to come because it was so weird to be in our new home.

Chapter 2

The next morning when I woke up, Mum came to tell me she was going to work, that the kids were ready, and we were going to go to the park at ten o'clock with the twins' friends and their mum, Abby. They lived on the floor above. That's one of the reasons Mum chose to move here. I gave her a quick hug before she left, then I dragged myself out of bed to eat the toast she'd left for me. "Hi kids," I said when I entered the living room, and they waved back. The twins were watching CBeebies, and Clover was playing with her rattle in her highchair. I quickly ate breakfast and got ready, then put the twins and Clover in their shoes and coats and we left the flat and made our way to the park that lies opposite. We crossed the road and the twins ran into the park after spotting their friends.

They played for hours until it started to pour with rain and a wind whipped up around us. All of a sudden, the park was deserted. Theo's coat had blown away in the wind and he was chasing after it so Abby took Andrea, Clover and both her kids back to her flat and told me to meet her there. Eventually Theo caught the coat and we ran from the park hand in hand. There was not a single soul in sight, not even a car on the road. That's when it happened.

The rain was so heavy it was impossible to see more than a few metres. Then Theo's hand slipped from mine. I thought he'd just fallen over so I leant down to haul him up and I fell too. But I didn't land with a thud on the road. I just kept falling through the air. I felt like I was going to keep falling forever.

Chapter 3

The temperature dropped rapidly as we fell and the hole we'd fallen through got smaller and smaller until it vanished completely, drowning us in darkness. I was surprised at how slowly we were falling. It was like someone had pressed a button to make everything go in slow motion. I suddenly stopped falling and thudded onto a cold, slimy floor. I sat up, astonished I hadn't been turned to mush on hitting the ground. To my left a dank slimy tunnel was dimly lit by spluttering gas lamps. "Theo!" I called out.

"Ember" he replied, scurrying over to me.

"What happened?" I gasped, enveloping my brother in a tight hug.

"Where are we?" Theo gulped.

He was trembling. I picked him up and saw the scared expression on his face. I wrapped him up in his coat even though it was sodden and told him, with uncertainty; "I'm sure it's fine. We just need to find someone that can help us."

"But there is no one down here," Theo whimpered.

Inside I agreed with him. Who on earth would be here? But I shook my head and replied; "Of course there is. Don't look so scared. Let's go and see if we can find someone."

"Ok..." Theo mumbled. I looked up just to make sure that there was no way of getting back up to the hole. Nope. There was no way we were getting back up there, even if someone threw down a rope ladder.

We wandered aimlessly in the gloom for hours. I occasionally glanced over my shoulder because I couldn't shake the feeling that something was following us. Eventually I gave up. "It's no use Theo. I'm sorry. We'll just have to stay here and hope that someone finds us. Mum will tell the police we've gone missing, and they'll use experts and trained dogs to sniff us out. It'll be alright." I slouched against one of the slimy walls and sighed. "Look Ember!" Theo pointed to something glinting far up ahead. He stood up and took my hand.
"What do you see Theo?"
"I see a...come on, let's go!" I was taken by surprise when he started running into the distance.
"Theo! Hold on!" I jumped up and charged after him, catching up easily. After a moment, I thought I saw something too. Not very clearly - it was just a little flash of golden light. It blinked on and off over and over again. Against my better judgement I decided to go and find out what it was. There was no point sitting in the dark waiting for someone to come and rescue us. Nobody even knew we were here yet.

We kept on running until we reached a... well, what actually was it!? It looked sort of like the eye of a storm, I guessed. It was different shades of purple and it swirled and boiled angrily in the air the front of us. I could feel it pulling me closer. I had to use all my strength to stay where I was.

"Stand back! You don't want to get pulled inside!" I said worriedly, sticking my hand out in front of him. We stood stock still and considered the sight in front of us. Now I knew what I'd seen glinting. Every so often a streak of gold light would zip across the purple clouds then vanish again.
"I want to go inside!" said Theo.

"Are you insane? We're not going through there. We might never come back!" I replied.
"But help might be in there!" he said.
"And so could a million and one deadly things! Come on, we're leaving," I told him. We were about to stride off when a horrible screaming sound echoed down the grimy passages. Theo gripped my hand, and I picked him up, ready to run for it. The scream stopped but then there was a different noise. Something was speaking to us.

"I know you're there children!" a menacing voice called. I froze. I swear even my blood stopped flowing. I could hear claws scraping against the tunnel floor. Whatever it was, it was getting closer. What the hell was it? I took a step back. Had it been following us this whole time? "Come out, come out wherever you are! I don't bite children!" The evil voice cackled.
Theo whispered something unintelligible in my ear and I backed away again even though it meant being perilously close to the purple storm. I could see a dark shadow approaching us, getting closer and closer.
"Ah. There you are children. Why were you hiding? Don't look so scared! Now come over here and I can introduce myself." I inched further backwards as the shadow crept closer. I could almost make out what it was now. It looked a bit like an alligator, but it was monstrous, completely black with blood red eyes and five spikes protruding from the tip of its tail. It screamed that awful scream again and began charging towards us, tail swinging and teeth bared. Just as we were about to get torn to shreds by those blade-like teeth, a hand thrust out of the purple clouds, grabbed my shoulder, and yanked us through backwards.

Chapter 4

There was a distant beeping sound and a bright light shone in my eyes, but my vision was too blurry to make anything out.
"I don't know," a man's voice was saying.
"Bring in Alora and Zandar, they should be able to sort something out." My vision was clearing, so I tried to sit up, but as soon as I did, I flopped back down again. My head was throbbing like mad and weighed a ton.
"Ah! Awake at last. It's only been two days!" said a smiling woman.
"Two days!" I began to panic. We'd been gone for two days? Mum would be losing her mind! Oh god, I thought. We need to get home!
"Do you think we should put her back to sleep again?" the woman was saying. "She's getting herself all worked up."
"No, no. I'm fine! Theo! Theo?" I waited for him to reply but he didn't. "Where's my brother?" I asked, looking round the room in a panic.
"It's fine, your brother is next door," somebody answered before putting something cold on my forehead and wrapping me up in a thin blanket.

Everything was becoming clearer, and I could make out where I was; on a lonely bed in a hospital room and I could see there were a neat line of stiches all up my arm. At that moment a boy and girl about my age sped into the room, out of breath and sweating. "Sorry...we took...so long," the girl panted.

"What is going on?" I shouted angrily, fed up with nobody telling me anything.

I looked around, scowling at the strange people surrounding me. The ones that I guessed were doctors nodded at the girl and boy and left. "Greetings," began the girl, who sat down beside of me. "My name is Alora; this is my friend Zandar. You are?"

"Ember," I replied.

"Pleasure to meet you!" Zandar grabbed my hand and shook it vigorously. "Welcome to Lowerground."

"Lowerground?" I repeated and Alora nodded. I laid in silence thinking about what had happened since me and Theo had fallen into this strange place. We'd trudged through those smelly, dank pipes for hours and hours, then seen the stormy purple portal and then that horrible black alligator. I couldn't remember anything after that. "How come I've been knocked out for two days?" I asked, eventually.

"You hit your head when you came through The Portal," answered Alora.

"Okay. And why do I have stiches all up my arm?"

"Because the Snapper caught you with its tooth just as you were pulled through The Portal," Zandar told me.

"Is a Snapper that weird black alligator thing that talked to me and my brother? How is that possible?" I asked.

"Yes, that's a Snapper. And they can talk because they were mutated in underground labs. But Storm will tell you all about that later," Zandar said.

"Where did you see the Snapper?" questioned Alora, sounding concerned.

"Right outside that purple storm thing."

"That's The Portal. The way into One from The Outside. There shouldn't be Snappers that close to The Portal. This can't be right."

This was all so much to take in. "So where am I? Lowerground, The Outside or One?" I asked, trying to set things straight in my mind.
"One, but One is in Lowerground," replied Zandar. "One is our city. There are four cities. One to Four, obviously. Think of it like this; Lowerground is our country and it has four cities. The Outside is everything that surrounds Lowerground, like the ocean surrounds an island." Putting it like that helped me to understand. Everything almost made sense now, other than the fact there was what seemed to be an entire civilisation living at the bottom of an abandoned sewage pipe.
"So how come there's like a whole world down here if you knew that Southampton was right above your heads?" I asked.
"Lowerground was actually here first. We've always been here, safe underground" answered Alora. "A few hundred years after Lowerground was built, some of our people ventured up to what we call the Above, where you come from, and decided to stay and build a new civilisation up there." I nodded and let the information sink in.

After a moment of quiet, I demanded "I want to see my brother".
"You will be permitted to see your brother at dinner tonight but don't worry, he's in good hands. Our finest nurse, Aster, is looking after him. In the meantime, we shall get you cleaned up." Alora replied. I nodded uncertainly but followed them out of the hospital room.

They took me to a huge bathroom. The walls and ceiling were white marble tiles and the floor was a slab of polished grey

rock. In the centre of the large room was a huge bath built into the floor full of bubbly water, which reminded me of a hot tub. There was an array of brightly coloured soaps in glass bottles lined up on the edge of the tub and a large, soft, cream towel hung on a hook by the door. Our whole flat would fit in here twice over, I thought.
"We'll leave you to wash and once you've finished, we'll take you to dinner," said Zandar, closing the door behind him as he and Alora left.

Until now I hadn't realised how dirty I was. Slimy green goo, presumably from the tunnels, coated me from head to toe. I stripped off and slid into the bath. The water was warm, and the bubbles were welcoming and I slowly began to relax. After a while of laying there and enjoying the sensation of warm bubbles, I thought I'd better scrub off all the slime and get out. I swam across to the other side of the deep bath and picked up the first bottle of soap. Inside the container was a thick lilac liquid which smelled fresh and wild. I scrubbed it into my hair until my scalp got sore, determined to get rid of all the grime. Next, I picked up a bottle full of mint green soap and rubbed it into every crevice of my body until I was sure I was clean, then washed it off.

Reluctantly, I climbed out of the bath and rubbed myself dry with the towel. I turned around to get dressed but found that my own clothes weren't there. Instead, there were a pair of emerald-green trousers, thick matching jacket and white shirt, socks, underwear, and shoes draped over a chair. I got dressed into the new clothes and tied my hair in loose braids before leaving the bathroom for dinner. "Ready?" asked Alora, who had been waiting outside. I nodded and followed her as she led the way to dinner.

Once we'd finally climbed to the top of a seemingly endless set of spiral stairs we rounded on a long corridor, framed by glass walls. I was getting more curious by the second.
"Where are we?" I asked.
"You're in our home, Peak. It's the beating heart of One," replied Zandar.
"You never really told me anything about One when I was in the hospital, or any of the other cities for that matter" I said.
"One is the first city you enter from the Outside. If you're lucky enough to get past the Snappers unharmed. They come from the underground labs in Three that were built illegally during the war. Anyway, Storm will tell you about that. Snappers are mutated alligators. Vicious and dangerous. You two are lucky my brother Sunday pulled you through The Portal before that Snapper got you," said Alora.
"Sunday?" I repeated. God, they had some weird names down here; Storm, Sunday, Zandar.
"Yes, my older brother. There he is now actually." We'd stopped at an enormous dining room. A huge glass table was placed in the middle and underneath our feet was an immaculate white carpet. To the left of the table were two pristine white armchairs and at the right side of the room sat a white desk and chair.

Alora was pointing directly at a young man only a little older than the three of us. He was tall and very handsome, with broad shoulders and rippling muscles. He had scruffy chocolate brown hair and a soft smiling expression. Like the rest of us he was wearing green trousers and a white shirt. This was Sunday. I felt my cheeks growing pink. Alora and Zandar strolled into the room and took their places at the table. I nervously trailed after them, feeling shy but brightening immediately when I saw Theo waving his chubby little hands at me. I took the seat next to Theo, sandwiched between him and Sunday. I whispered questions to him about what had happened since we'd been here while everyone else around the table murmured to one another.

Chapter 5

All of a sudden, a man aged about fifty rose from his seat and the burble of hushed chatter from around the table ceased. “Good evening, we have all assembled in the Cabin” (I assumed that’s what this room was called) “to discuss something very important. Time for some introductions first, I think. I’m Storm, President of One, or as some like to call it, The Shining city.” He pointed out of the window. “Come to me if you have any questions.” I spun around on my chair and looked out of the window. I saw far below us an enormous city. The buildings, some tall, some short, were all white and perfect just like the room we were sitting in. The pavements were spotless and glossy. It looked like an immaculate maze of buildings, so cramped you could hardly breathe, but I noticed towards the edge of the city everything thinned out and there were only a few buildings dotted about. The whole city was a perfect circle and Peak was the tallest building by far, and dead in the centre. Storm let me admire his city for a moment before moving on.

“Now, I’m led to believe you’ve already met Alora and Zandar, the two best engineers in One. Don’t let their age fool you.”
“Yes, I’ve met them,” He nodded and then continued.
“Next, we have Aster. She has been looking after your brother since you arrived and is the finest nurse at our hospital which

is based here in Peak. Peak is also where the army trains and is home to those whose work is based here. Basically, everything important happens here. Sunday is the last person I wanted you to meet tonight. He's the star member of the army. I'm sure you'll get on like a house on fire.

"As most of you will already know, two arrivals from the Above were pulled through The Portal just as they were about to get caught by a Snapper. Thankfully Sunday was patrolling the area, after we had received intel that the Snappers were prowling." He pointed his forefinger at me and Theo. "These are our arrivals. Now, what are your names?"
"Ember," I replied, "and this is my brother, Theo."
"Ember..." he looked lost in thought and then, as if something had clicked in his mind, he spoke again; "She must be the girl from the prophecy!" and everyone around the table nodded.
"What?" I asked.
"Someone show her the prophecy," Storm demanded. One of the people from around the table went over to a cabinet and took out a large, ancient looking book, the brown leather cover peeling at the corners. They plonked it down on the table and flicked through until they reached the last page and turned it around so I could read what it said. It said something or other about victory and justice, but at the bottom of the page, which was torn and ragged, it read:

'Watch for the girl with fire inside of her, because she will be both the saviour and destroyer of Lowerground.

"What does this mean?" I asked.

"It means you are the girl the prophecy speaks of!" Storm said excitedly.

"I still don't get what you mean." I replied, "how can you tell just from that sentence?"
"Because only someone from Lowerground or someone with extreme power can see and use our magical Portal to access our world. Aside from than that, your name is Ember and in the prophecy it says; *watch for the girl with fire inside of her.* Don't you see? Ember...fire?" I started to understand what he was talking about. I just couldn't believe that I had any special powers.

Storm continued "Long, long ago when Lowerground was new, all four cities lived in peace, united as equals. But after living peacefully side by side for several hundred years, Three decided they wanted to be the ruling city. To accomplish this they built laboratories under their city and began mutating the alligators that lived in The Outside. They worked in great secrecy and nobody suspected anything was amiss. That was until half the population of Four disappeared. Three had let Snappers into the city through the long-abandoned pipes that we used to use to send goods from city to city. We couldn't let them get away with it, so One, Two and what was left of Four waged war against Three. It was a long and bloody battle, and we lost a lot of good people, but in the end we were victorious.

"After the war all the cities decided to cut off all contact with each other as we'd lost our trust in each other. However, even after we'd defeated Three, they kept the Snappers under their control. We suspect they've mutated more species since the war, waiting for the next time they can use them in battle. After many generations, Four recovered but things have never been the same in Lowergound. You are the girl from the prophecy Ember, and I believe you will save One, Two and Four and destroy Three! Unfortunately, we don't have the slightest clue how."

Everyone began chattering again and ordering food and drinks. I sat stock still, my head spinning, unable to process what was happening. A plate of food was pushed in front of me and someone shook my shoulder to focus my attention. I looked down at the plate and grimaced. There was some sort of meat, at least, that's what I thought it was. It was dark pink and edged with a magenta crust. Yellow shoots, purple peas and orange bread also decorated my plate. I looked at Theo, who was looking back at me with the same confused yet hungry expression. "It won't be too bad," I whispered to him, "On the count of three we'll try some, okay?" He nodded. This is what Mum did when he refused to eat his vegetables. "One, two, three." We both took a mouthful of peas. They had an odd crunchy texture but tasted okay. The woman to the left of Theo suddenly started talking to him and encouraging him to eat up. I wasn't sure I liked this but had to let it slide because Storm started talking again. "How do you feel about staying here for a while then Ember?" he questioned.

"What? You mean we can't go home?" I asked.

"It's not to say that you can't, it's that we daren't let you. We need you here. You are destined to be both the saviour and destroyer of Lowerground."

"But what about our family? Our mum will be worried sick. Please! Anything, even if it's just a letter telling her where we are?" I begged, rage bubbling inside me.

"No, I'm afraid not. With all of that covered, I have one last thing to say. Tomorrow we will gather here again to let you meet some more important members of the team who couldn't make it tonight and discuss our future plans. I'll be ready and waiting at nine thirty, so don't be late. Ember, Alora and Zandar will take you to your living quarters. I hope they meet your standards. Goodnight." Storm finished.

I wasn't quite sure what to say. My mind whirled with all the information I'd just taken in. How everyone in the Lowerground was led to believe that I was supposed to save and destroy their entire world. And that they wouldn't let us go home.

Taking Theo's hand, I followed Alora and Zandar down chilly marble corridors until we reached a door printed with the number 407 at the top. I was too tired to do anything but take a quick look at the room, slip on a white robe and slide under the sheets. It took me a while to go to sleep because so many thoughts were rushing through my mind that it must have been early morning by the time I dropped off.

Chapter 6

I slept for a few hours and woke up with a start. Theo was sleeping soundly on the bed to my right which forced my mind to relax a little. I turned to the left and found Alora quietly snoring and, on the farthest bed from mine, Zandar sprawled on his back. There was a small clock on the wall which told me it was six thirty. I sighed and slid out of bed, knowing there was no chance I was going back to sleep. Still rubbing the sleep from my eyes, I yawned and turned on a lamp, hoping it wouldn't rouse anyone. The lamp provided little light, but it was bright enough to let me see where I was going as I crept around my new living quarters. I found a small bathroom, kitchen and a living-room with two large, curved sofas.

Not sure what else to do, I pulled on the shoes I was given last night and slipped soundlessly out of the door. I stood in the corridor thinking things over. There were only two places, other than my living area, that I'd been to since the hospital. The Cabin and that huge bathroom. Thinking I could do with another wash, I tried to navigate my way to the bathroom but ended up having to ask one of Storm's servants to take me.

After relaxing in the bath, I got dressed into the outfit I'd worn yesterday and left the bathroom. The same servant that had escorted me to the bathroom told me that it was about seven in the morning. There was still ages until the meeting with Storm in the Cabin, so I went off to find the stairs that would take me to the bottom floor. After a while of wandering, I found them and jogged down to the ground floor and escaped through the glass doors out into the fresh air.

It was cold this early in the morning, and I wished I'd remembered to bring my jacket. The city was silent and still and I seemed to be the only one awake. Without a destination in mind, I began to wander around the city. I looked through windows, went down dark alleyways and found myself at the very edge of the city.

To my great surprise and confusion, when I reached the edge of the city, the sky seemed to come down and meet the ground. But of course, this couldn't be the sky because we were underground. I hadn't really given this much thought until now. I'd been walking around One in early morning sunlight this whole time and it had not clicked that there couldn't be real sunlight beneath the sewers. Feeling muddled, I thought hard and realised that the 'sky' had to be a dome and that the images of the rising sun in a blue sky were programmed onto it. Feeling curious, I stretched out my hand and felt a tingling sensation in my fingers as they passed through the dome. Determined to know what lay waiting on the other side, I pushed my whole hand through and the tingling danced from my fingertips to my wrist. It was like having pins and needles. For a moment I thought of pushing my face through so I could at least see what lie in the darkness behind it, but realised I might as well just step through and see what happened. I would only go for a second mind you, I couldn't just leave Theo here and run off. I looked back at the city, not liking how I was trapped and the fact that even the sky wasn't real down here. I was about to step through when-

"I wouldn't do that if I were you," I turned around to see Sunday giving me a judgemental look.

"Why not?" I replied, trying to hide my shock at being discovered.

"Because once you leave, there's no coming back," Sunday answered.

"How dramatic," I shot back, rolling my eyes. "Besides, I wasn't planning on running away, I just wanted to know what was on the other side." Sunday stared at me in silence for a moment, then opened his mouth like he was about to say something then closed it again. You look like a fish out of water when you do that, I thought inside my head, but didn't quite dare say.

"You'd better pull your arm back through," he said.

"If you say so," I replied nonchalantly, secretly glad he'd suggested it. I was thoroughly hating the feeling of pins and needles. I pulled my arm back through and found that everything up to my elbow was completely numb. I shook my arm about hoping to restore the feeling.

"Follow me," Sunday said suddenly.

"Why? Where are we going?" I asked suspiciously.

"You'll see. Come on, let's go."

Against my better judgement, I obediently went after him. We strode along the outskirts of the city trying not to make eye contact until we reached our destination. "Ta da!" said Sunday, "we have arrived." I looked up at the abandoned building that towered above me. It was made from dirty grey concrete unlike the rest of the polished glass skyscrapers back in the centre of One and weeds grew out of cracks in the crumbling cement. "Ready?" Sunday asked.

"Ready for wh-?" Before I could finish my sentence, he'd started scrabbling up the side of the building. He was using windowsills and holes in the concrete as foot and hand holds. I quickly copied him. "Hey!" I called up to him, angrily, "you could have warned me that you were going to do that, you know!"
"Calm down, we're only just off the ground." He gave me a mischievous grin and began to clamber the rest of the way to the top. Any interest I'd felt for him last night had vanished. Without thinking about what I was doing I followed him up, wanting to prove that I was just as good at climbing as he was. "Come on, slowcoach!" he called down to me after he'd reached the top.
"Shut up, show-off!" I shouted back.

Once I'd reached the top, I found him sitting down near the edge, waiting for me. I walked across the chunks of broken concrete and sat down next to him.
I was even colder up here and goosebumps prickled my arms.
"Here," Sunday said, putting his jacket around my shoulders.
"Thanks," I replied. "Why'd you bring me up here?"
"This is where I go to be alone. No-one comes here and I need to tell you some stuff you should probably know. It's pretty brutal down here, I just thought I'd give you a heads up."
"Thanks. But I thought Storm would do that sort of stuff," I replied.
"Wrong. Storm tells you what he wants you to know. Like about the history of Lowerground, that sort of stuff. Anything else is considered classified."
"Oh. So there's lots of secrets?" I asked, interested.
"I guess you could say that."
"Come on then, tell me what there is to know." I commanded.
"Okay pushy. I guess the first thing you should know is about the Defts" he began.
"Defts?" I cut in, "what are those?"

"I was about to tell you. Defts are people who were exiled after the war. I don't know why though. Storm did a good job covering that up. You shouldn't trust him."
"Don't worry, I don't," I replied.
"Good. Anyway," he continued, "Once you go through the Dome, there's no coming back. All the Defts live out there. Rumour has it that they've built other cities. Just like One. But no-one's ever seen one so we can't be sure."
"And why do I need to know this?" I asked.
"Because, you never know when you might be able use this information," Sunday replied.
"Good thinking." I paused for a moment before asking; "Any more secrets you want to tell me?"
"Hmmmm," Sunday pondered, "Actually, yes, there is something else. I didn't want to tell you at first, but I don't see the point in hiding anything from you. You're not safe down here, Ember. Three know about the prophecy too and they want you in their clutches and if they can't have you, they'll kill you…" he trailed off.
"Thanks for the heads up. That makes me feel really safe." We sat staring out at One. All the glass skyscrapers sparkled in the morning sunlight.

"It must be nice to live down here. Everything is so perfect," I said, breaking the silence.
"Eh? It may seem nice down here, but I'd choose the Above any day," replied Sunday.
"I dunno. There's always so many wars, a million horrible people, litter, seagulls. I could go on forever."
"Well yeah, there's gonna be bad stuff but what about all the nice parts? Like forests, lakes, theme parks?"
"I suppose that stuff's cool. But aren't there nice things down here too?" I asked.
"Nope."

"So you're telling me that you've never been for a walk through the trees or swum in a lake before?" I asked in disbelief.

"I am. There's no nature down here. No fun stuff. No nothing. Well, unless you count skyscrapers. I've never left this place. Not once in my entire life. I'm not going to either unless I get taken on an army mission where we have to enter another city. I'm stuck here for good," he said, gloomily.

"I can't imagine living down here my whole life. I can't imagine never seeing the real sun, moon or stars, or a rainbow. Or never going out in the rain or building a snowman. Never going to the beach, a park, or sailing across the water on a boat..." my voice trailed off as a million and one memories flooded my mind. So many happy days. Rain or shine. Wind or snow. I doubted I'd ever make another memory like that. I'd be stuck down here forever. Trapped, like Sunday.

I saw Sunday's brow furrow as he tried to imagine all these things. "Believe me, I wish I had experienced all those things." he sighed before saying; "We'd better be getting back to Peak now. Let's go. Storm will lose it if we're late for the meeting." I nodded and we both descended, using the same technique as before.

Once back on the ground, we strolled back to Peak, occasionally exchanging awkward snatches of conversation, and reached the Cabin right on time for the meeting. I gave him a coy smile, shrugged off his jacket and passed it back to him. He nodded at me, entered the Cabin, and took his seat at the table. I was about to follow him when Alora sped round the corner and interrogated me on where I'd been and what I'd been doing. She reached up to brush cement dust out of my hair and said "I'm supposed to be looking after you Ember. You're not making this easy for me." I smiled and apologised and together we went through the doorway and took our seats.

Chapter 7

I sat down and had a quick chat with Theo as a breakfast of yellow toast and green jam was wheeled in. It looked less weird than last night's meal, so I took a sip of water and began to eat, suddenly realising how hungry I was. "Morning everyone," Storm began, "let's get straight to the point as everyone around this table has duties they must attend to. Let's do the introductions. This is my assistant." Storm pointed to a pretty, young woman with long blonde hair and circular glasses.

"Hello," she said. She spoke to Theo and me in a voice you might use if you were cooing at a baby or a puppy. "I'm Candace. I'm basically in charge of all the paperwork and make sure Storm has everything he needs." I nodded and turned my attention to the man next to her.

"I'm Zale, commanding officer of our army. I train our best men and women and they give our city maximum protection." It looked like years of being a commanding officer had hardened and scarred his face and turned his voice to a deep snarl. I decided that I didn't like him all too much. The next two people were twins, Ruben and Riggs, both very different in looks. Riggs, head of the police force, was tall and muscular with a shiny black crew cut and a stern expression which told me you didn't mess with him. On the other hand, Ruben was very jolly and had a blonde beard and full head of hair. "My job is to distribute food to the people of our city." he informed me.

"Isn't there enough food?" I asked.

"Not recently. In Four, the city where most of our food comes from, all the crops failed last harvest because Three released a virus into their soil which then poisoned all the livestock. So we're living on basic rations." replied a girl about my age with short blue hair and a mischievous glint in her eye. "Hi, I'm Neptune by the way. I'm one of the spies. I sneak into Three and make sure they aren't up to anything," she winked at me, and I knew I could trust her.

"It was a bit stupid to poison all the food because now they have nothing to eat either," I thought aloud.

"Oh, they have food. They've been storing it in their underground labs for years. They're trying to kill us off," a girl with shoulder length green hair told me. "The name's Pluto. I develop the weapons that we're going to be using in the war."

"War?" I said, alarmed.

"Yes. War." Storm cut in, "We are going to war again. We got the message last night. As it was all those years ago, we are going to ally ourselves with Two and Four. Four have discovered that Three released mutated snakes into the Outside yesterday morning. The Snappers also grow bolder. We are no longer safe and must do all in our power to protect the citizens. Riggs, get out there with the police force and start alerting the citizens, but try not to alarm them," Riggs nodded and dashed out of the room. "Zale and Sunday, gather up the rest of the troops, tell them what's happening and start training. We will need all your talents later." They both rose from their seats and jogged down the hall. "Pluto, Alora and Zandar-I need you to prepare as many weapons as you can. Go! Candace with me to the Communication Room. Lastly Theo and Ember, can you remember the way back to your room? I know it may seem that you are useless at the moment, but I trust that later on you will be our greatest, most lethal weapon. Now off you go."

I wasn't sure I liked the sound of that. We both got up from the table and made our way down the hall. I felt glad that we didn't have any duties to attend to and got to go and relax but I couldn't actually remember the way back to our room. Never mind, I thought, we can just wander around until we find it. "So," I said to Theo as we turned down a deserted corridor, hand in hand, "how are you feeling? We haven't seen much of each other have we?" I asked.
"No, we haven't. I'm okay but I miss Mummy and Andrea. Not Clover. She wakes me up EVERY night." he replied.
"Yes, it was nice not having to listen to her crying last night," I pictured my little sister crying. In my imagination, Mum came in to sort her out and ended up sitting by Clover's cot and crying as well. Missing us. Thinking we're dead. Wanting us to come home more than anything. This thought was too much to bear, and I immediately forced it from my mind. If only Mum knew we were alright. If only she knew where we were.
"I miss Mummy and Drea too, but we'll get home soon, I promise."

But that was a promise I couldn't keep. At that moment a distinctly familiar shriek echoed down the hall. I looked around to find the source of the sound, but the corridor was still completely empty. Theo gripped my hand and we began to quicken our pace. There was silence and then the piercing scream erupted from directly around the approaching corner. I knew I'd heard that sound before. "Run!" I yelled. Panicked, frightened and confused Theo let go of my hand and ran as fast as he could. "Theo!" I called. But he didn't turn back. He'd always been like this. Whenever he was scared, he'd run away from everyone, feeling embarrassed. All of a sudden, the lights burnt out and I was swept off my feet and onto the cold scaly backs of a throng of charging Snappers.

Chapter 8

I bounced up and down on the Snapper's back as they stampeded in pursuit of Theo. "Theo!" I yelled. I had to get free and rescue him. I tried to get my balance and stand up only to lurch backwards and fall to the ground as the Snappers surged onward. "Hurry!" shouted the leading Snapper in its strange, malicious voice.

"But we've lost the girl, Dagon!" one of them called back.

"Never mind that! If we have the boy she'll come and rescue him. We'll use him as bait. Now, pick up the pace, he's getting away!" Dagon shouted back, "Let's just get the boy and return to Three!"

"No! Run, Theo. I'm coming!" I shouted. I picked myself off the floor and bolted after them. Up ahead I saw the great glass wall of the skyscraper approaching. Theo was almost there. He would have nowhere else to run. With one final shriek, Dagon sank his teeth into Theo's back and Theo crumpled to the floor in pain. "Theo!" I yelled, using all my strength to try to get to him. But I couldn't. Dagon, using his blade-like teeth, had picked Theo up and flicked him onto his back, then charged straight through the glass wall. "No, come back!"

"Ember!" screamed Theo. I got one last look at his face before he disappeared from sight. His eyes were wide with panic and tears were streaming down his red cheeks.

I couldn't let this happen. I wouldn't let this happen. Even though I was weak from exhaustion and fear, I used the last of my energy and went after him. I got to the smashed window and looked down; the Snappers were running through the maze of buildings that made up the city, heading in the direction of The Portal. People screamed and dodged out of their way, but nobody was brave enough to save the helpless little boy riding on their backs. Without giving any thought to the consequences, prepared to do everything in my power to get to my brother, even if it meant a brutal end, I jumped. Only after I launched myself into the air, did I realise what I had done and what would closely follow. A human pancake. A bloody mess. A dark red stain that would never really be erased from the perfect white paths of One. Pedestrians who were already in hysteria at the sight of Theo being carried away by Dagon and his army, screamed as they saw what I'd done. I looked down in panic and gasped my last breath. But much to my surprise, I wasn't falling. What? I thought, feeling relieved and baffled as something tightened around my wrist. I heard a sigh of relief pass through the crowd, and I looked up to see Sunday. He was grasping my wrist with his right hand and his left hand was hanging onto the ledge. What? I asked myself again. Sunday hardly knew me. We'd only just met. Why would he risk his life trying to save mine? I felt Sunday's arm tremble. No wonder, he was holding the weight of two fairly heavy people. I felt my wrist begin to slip through his fingers as his grip weakened from the weight he was holding. I tried to grasp a hold of him, but I couldn't. My fingers couldn't grab hold of his wrist in time. "Ember!" shouted Sunday as we slid apart. I looked up at his face, the last thing I'd ever see. I couldn't decide how he was feeling. Angry at himself for not being able to hold on? Angry at me for jumping? Scared and sad that the saviour and destroyer of Lowerground was dead? I guessed I'd never know.

I took one last breath and felt the world shatter around me, like the fragile glass I'd just leapt through.

Chapter 9

Beep. Beep. Beep.

I couldn't remember a thing. Not one thing about my whole life. Not my name. Not how old I was, nor where I was. Nothing made sense. Worry and pain stabbed me all over. I tried to speak, to say something, to ask what was happening, but as soon as I opened my mouth a hot liquid dribbled out and ran down my chin. It tasted metallic, of iron, of blood. I opened my eyes, desperate and disoriented. My vision was blurred and all I could make out were blobs of white and peach hurrying around the room, exchanging snatches of conversation that I couldn't understand. The fear and frustration that I felt was overpowering. When I tried to move, I found I couldn't. I looked down at myself feeling panicky, only to find that white plaster covered every inch of my body. Suddenly I was being lifted into an upright position and realised I was on a bed in a hospital. Then, somebody sat down opposite me, with a very gentle look on her face. Her face-I recognised it! But who was she to me? A friend, my sister? That made me think, did I even have a sister or brother? Where were my parents? Maybe this woman was my mother? I had so many questions that I couldn't ask, fearing more blood would flow if I opened my mouth. And I couldn't hear properly, so even if I could ask, I wouldn't be able to hear the answer. Luckily, the woman seemed to

understand all of this. She came and squeezed some drops of medicine into my eyes and after a few moments the world wasn't so blurry anymore. Next, she wrote something down on a piece of paper and brought it over to me.
"Could you try to speak again?" it said on the paper. I opened my mouth and began choking on blood. The woman forced some water down my throat, and I stopped choking. "Good", she wrote, "keep trying". So, I did. My voice was barely a whisper, I had to strain to say every syllable and my throat burned. But I didn't stop. "Wh-at... ha-p-pen-ed?" I croaked. Before answering, the woman crossed the room, picked up a large bottle of brown liquid and shoved a spoonful down my throat. It tasted awful and was hard to swallow.
"That should have helped your hearing. Has it worked?" I nodded. "Excellent. Now what was your question? Ah, yes. What happened was that you jumped from a skyscraper. We thought you were dead. You're extremely lucky to be alive Ember." she told me. Ember. That was me. An unusual name, I thought, but nice all the same. Anticipating what my next question was going to be, she then said, "You were chasing after the Snappers that took your brother. You didn't think before jumping." So I did have a brother and I was trying to save him. I still had so many questions though. What were Snappers, why did they want my brother, where was he now? Again, she seemed to know what I wanted to ask and explained to me "Snappers are basically super smart mutated alligators. They took your brother to Three, one of the four cities of Lowerground, because they need you to win this war. I imagine they plan to use him as bait." There was so much to take in, but I was starting to remember little things now. Like where I was for instance; in One. I remembered how I was such an important piece in the ongoing war between the four cities. And that this kind woman was called Aster. But that was about it. The only thing I could really think about right now was the unimaginable pain I felt in

every bone in my body. "Wh-at's w-wrong w-ith m-m-me?" I asked.
"Let's see, both of your arms and legs were broken but not to worry, they are well on the mend. You fractured your skull and damaged a few vertebrae. You had ruptured your spleen, but we've had that removed, you can live without that. Lastly, you punctured one lung, but again, not to worry, we're fixing that. A long list I know, but you will recover." I went over the list of injuries in my mind and marvelled at the fact I was still alive. "Now Ember, it's important that you remember as much about yourself as possible so we'll call in one of your friends to see if they can jog your memory and I'll tell you a bit more about yourself. Only if you're up to it however. I don't want to exhaust you," offered Aster.
"Y-es p-ple-ase," I whispered back, desperate to remember everything.
"Okay. You're fifteen years old, you come from Southampton, and you and your brother Theo have been in Lowerground for four months," she tells me. Fifteen years. I'd forgotten fifteen years' worth of memories. I'd forgotten everything. Would I ever get those memories back? "My brother?"
"Yes?" prompted Aster.
"D-id I s-save him af-ter I ju-mped?"
"Unfortunately not," sighed Aster.
"So where is he?" I asked, inwardly fuming. I totally destroyed my body, and it didn't even achieve anything!
"He is being held hostage in Three."
"Well how are we going to get him back?" I questioned.
"Honestly, Ember, I don't know. In the meantime, how about I get someone to come and talk to you?" She said this as if it was going to make up for the fact that my brother wasn't here, but I agreed anyway.

"Right! I'll call for someone to come and see you." She strode off and left me alone with my thoughts of home and how long

I'd been down here. Four months. That was sinking in now. Me and my brother had been away from home for four months. Lowerground had been at war for four months. And I'd been out cold, almost dead, for the most part of it.

At that moment, Aster and a tall, handsome, young man entered the hospital room. "I'll leave you to chat with her for a while," Aster told him before stepping out the door. The young man sat down on the bed at my feet, careful not to touch my plaster cast.

"I'm so sorry, Ember." he said to me in his husky voice. This took me by surprise. I wasn't expecting an apology from anyone, why would I be? I just assumed he'd come and sit with me, maybe ask me what I remembered and try to 'jog my memory' like Aster had said.

"S-so-rry f-for...wh-at?" I croaked. He appeared distressed by the sound of my voice.

"For not being able to hold on," he replied after a second. Obviously, I looked confused, so he continued; "I dropped you remember." This is clearly a sensitive topic for him because he's speaking so quietly and looked as if all of this was his fault. "No, I d-don't rem-em-b-ber." I answered. He sighed because he was going to have to explain what happened. "I'm Sunday, do you remember me?" he asked, changing the subject.

"No," I said again. "A-are y-you m-m-my b-roth-er or s-something?" I stuttered.

"No. We only just met each other. I didn't really get the chance to know you before, well..." he pointed at my full body cast.

"Oh. I-if we'd o-only ju-st met, why d-did you want to s-save m-me?" I asked.

"I don't know." His cheeks suddenly had a red glow, and I knew this was a lie, but I didn't have the energy to argue. Neither of us said anything for a while and then I asked; "H-

how was this your f-ault?" My speech seemed clearer and it was easier for me to talk. "I j-jumped, d-didn't I?"
"Yeah, but then I caught you… and dropped you." Sunday replied.
"So, it's not your fault. T-his w-would have happened w-whether you dropped me or not. It could be much worse," and by that, I meant dead. Sunday nodded and seemed to feel a bit better when I told him this. "How come I'm not dead though? Falling from halfway up a building and landing on concrete is sure to kill you," I asked. My voice was still strained and husky but at least I could get out my words.
"We've got crazy medicines here. The doctors can cure almost anything. Besides, you only fell a couple of floors," Sunday replied. After a while, he spoke again in a surprisingly shy tone of voice. "So," he began, "Do you remember when I took you up to the roof of that crumbling old building?" I racked my brain, which gave me a headache, trying to remember what Sunday was talking about. And there it was. I remembered! Not very clearly, but still! I thought about that time. When we sat together under the projection of the morning sun. It must have been important to me, important enough to remember.
"Yeah, I remember." He smiled and, for the first time since he'd arrived, the lines on his forehead disappeared.
"Do you think the war will go on for much longer?" I asked.
"Yes. Wars aren't won overnight, Ember." I nodded disappointed. There was not much else to say after that. "Get well soon. We need you out there." Sunday planted a kiss on my forehead and left. I smiled. I couldn't remember what it felt like to be kissed. It felt nice.

After that Aster came in and put me back to sleep. When I woke up again, it was four weeks later.

Chapter 10

"Afternoon, sunshine," said Aster, gently. I didn't feel like sunshine. My head was heavy, and my mind was jumbled. I rolled over, wanting to go back to sleep and escape back into my dreams of my own world, where I lived a normal life in Southampton. Then I realised I could roll over. I opened my eyes and rubbed them. My arms were free! I looked down and found that the plaster had been removed and I was wearing a white hospital gown. I looked to Aster for confirmation that I was really free of the horrible itchy cast, and she nodded. I experimented with sitting and I could, though not easily. "Feeling any better?"

I took a minute to assess how I was feeling. I could move, which was great, I could hear perfectly again, and I could remember snippets of my past.

"Much better," I answered, finding that my voice was no longer strained.

"I thought you would," said Aster, perching on the edge of the bed. "Your body has had time to heal, and we've been giving you lots of medicines that are supposed to help you remember things. Do you think they've worked?" she asked.

"A little, yes," I replied.

"We've obviously given you lots of other treatments, but I don't want to bore you with the details. Now, as you'll probably realise, you'll never fully recover from this, you

understand Ember? There are going to be some things that you'll never remember no matter how hard you try. Some of your bones will never fully heal so may cause you some pain, but all the serious injuries are mended. Okay?"
It wasn't okay. It would never be okay, but I nodded anyway. I wondered what the things that I'd never be able to remember were. What if it was something important?
"Hungry?" Aster asked.
"What? Oh yes. I can't remember the last time I ate anything," I replied.
"Just as I thought, I'll bring you something now." She hurried off and returned with a bowl of bright purple stew and pink bread. I couldn't remember food being these colours back home. Aster told me that all the food down here was different colours compared to the Above. That's because there's no real sunlight in Lowerground so all the crops grow differently. I nodded and dug into the purple stew, suddenly fiendishly hungry.

After I'd scoffed the whole stew and licked the bowl clean, I was given a glass of water, and a white top with emerald green jacket and trousers. I remembered wearing these when me and my brother, what was his name… Th… Theo, first arrived here. I gulped down the water and slowly got dressed. "Want to go for a walk? You need to stretch out your muscles and get a feel for walking again," Aster asked.
"Sure," I replied standing up. I tried taking a step forward and found my legs were weak and stiff, along with the rest of me. I almost fell flat on my face, but Aster caught me. "Oh," I sighed. I decided I wasn't going to shuffle around in public looking like a robot, so I flopped back down on the bed, disheartened that I'd forgotten how to walk.
"Come on, Ember. I know it's hard, but you've got to try." Aster pulled me back up and helped me take stiff steps to the

door. She pulled the handle and led me out of the warm, safe hospital room and into a cool, bright reception room.
As soon as the door closed behind us, somebody threw herself at me and cried; "Ember!"
This was awkward. We obviously knew each other but I had no memory what-so-ever of this girl.
"Ummm...hello, who are you?" I questioned prising the girl off my neck.
"What? I'm Alora, who else would it be? We've been worried sick this whole time! We thought you were dead!" she was talking so fast, and overwhelming me, so I decided to just block her out and make my way to the glass door with my stiff, weak shuffle. "Ember! Where are you going?" she said, coming after me and grabbing my hand. "You can't go out there! It's not safe."
"What? Why not, how is it not safe? I need to go out, I need some fresh air," I told her.
"We're at war, remember? Three spies recently planted Blocks. When a Block senses movement it blows up or floods the air within a ten-metre radius with toxic gas. They're planted all over the city, you can't leave this building!" she said, tugging me away from the automatic door. This was bad.
Now come on, Storm wants to see you." She dragged me by my wrist past Aster, who I gave a pleading look to, and then up flights and flights of stairs.

"I don't think I'm meant to walk this far so soon. It's only the first time I've been out of bed in, like, five months or something," I told Alora after we'd started on the tenth flight of stairs.
"Nonsense," she answered, "If we were going any slower, we wouldn't be moving, it'll be fine."
"Isn't there a lift or something?" I asked.

"Yes, there is, but it's out of order. Hurry up!" She was talking to me like I was a stupid child who couldn't understand anything unless it was said in a loud and slow voice. Angrily, I followed after her.

Chapter 11

We finally arrived at the top floor and Alora took me into a room I vaguely remembered. I was pretty sure it was called the Cabin, or something like that. When we entered, I saw a crowd of people sitting around a table. They all looked up at me as I came through the door. "Ember," said the man sitting at the head of the table. I didn't like him, that I remembered all too well. I thought he was named after the weather or something ridiculous like that. He gave me a quick smile which I did not return. Alora sat me in the chair next to him. On my other side sat the tall and handsome boy, what was his name again?... Sunday!

"Feeling better?" he asked me.

"A little," I said.

"Wonderful, we've all been very worried about you, haven't we?" the man said. The people around the table all agreed. I thought I recognised some of their faces but couldn't for the life of me remember who they were. "Did Alora tell you about the Blocks, Ember? Great! Pluto," he pointed to a girl with bright green hair, "and her team are trying to find a way to deactivate the Blocks but no luck so far. Anyway, Zale has a grand plan to share with us. Take it away, Zale."

In a flash of inspiration, I suddenly remembered all of the names of the people around the table- Ruben, Riggs, Neptune,

Pluto, Sunday, Alora, and Storm. I couldn't help feeling like someone was missing, though. I swear there had always been a boy hanging out with Alora. What was his name? Zeke? Zane? Something like that. When I pulled myself away from my thoughts, I found that Zale had begun to speak.

"So," he said, "I have planned for an elite team of soldiers to invade Three in two days. This will give us time to prepare. My plan is that they will break into Three's Headquarters and take a few captives. We shall then torture them for information. We'll go straight from the Training Centre with weapons and gas masks in case we set off any of the Blocks. That shouldn't happen, though, because Pluto has been working on a way to detect the Blocks, so we should be able to avoid them." Zale crossed to a small cabinet and took out two large maps printed on blue paper. He then went on in detail about all his plans with everyone asking a question or two and appearing to be totally oblivious to anything but the blue maps. My attention was slowly slipping though, and I drifted off into my own world. I was thinking about my life back in Southampton, not that I remembered much of it. When Theo and I fell down here during the storm, after moving into the flat...Theo! It suddenly hit me that my brother was in Three, where the army would be going in a matter of days!

"My brother," I suddenly shouted, interrupting Zale. Everyone's gaze turned to me and Zale said "Yes, what about your brother?"

"Aren't you going to rescue him? He's in Three isn't he?" I asked.

"It's not exactly a priority," Zale answered.

"What? How can he not be a priority?" I protested, angrily. It seemed totally wrong to just leave him alone in Three. I begged and shouted at them for ten minutes straight, but they didn't concede to rescuing him.

"Fine," I yelled. "but his blood is on your hands. If anything happens to him, I blame you!" Nobody seemed to care. I racked my mind for something that would make them rethink. Then it clicked. "Aren't I meant to be busy saving and destroying Lowerground? If you want my help with that, I suggest you get me my brother!"

"You seem to have a selective memory, Ember. You can't remember your own name but when it comes to something that you can benefit from, your mind is crystal clear," said Storm. Taken aback, I disagreed but he just scoffed.

"At the moment you're useless to us Ember," Storm said after musing over my argument. "No-one really knows what that prophecy means and until we figure out how to use you, stay silent. Besides, Zale's right, Theo isn't a priority. We'll work on getting him back soon."

Not sure what else to do I stood up and stormed out of the room. If they wouldn't get Theo back, I would. I thought to myself. Luckily, I knew when Zale and the rest of the army were planning to break into Three, so I'd just have to sneak along with them. I waited until everyone had left the Cabin and then dashed back in and opened the cabinet that Zale took the blue maps from. As I'd suspected, the maps had been put back in, so I took them out and laid them on the meeting table. I planned to go to the Training Centre first and find a weapon to defend myself with against the Snappers when I made it into the Outside. I shuddered at the memory of the Snappers. I wished I didn't remember them. On the first map, which was of Peak, I found the ninth floor was labelled 'Training Centre' and decided that first thing tomorrow I'd make my way there. The second map showed all of Three, everything I'd need to find Theo, and go and break him out. Hopefully. I turned to leave, keeping the map of Three and jumped because Sunday was leaning on the doorframe.

"Planning something I see," he said. I tried to push past him, but he purposely blocked my path.
"I'm not planning anything and even if I was it's none of your business," I said, accepting that I was not getting past him.
"Okay! But if you need any help with whatever you're not planning, you know where to find me. And by the way, those maps are very inaccurate, so they won't be much help," and with that he sauntered off.
"Thanks, but I won't be coming to find you," I said to myself before creeping off to the hospital room where I'd been sleeping for the past five months.

Chapter 12

I knocked on the door to my hospital room after taking the stairs down to the first floor. Aster opened the door and seemed surprised, "Hello," she said, in an inquisitive tone.
"Hi," I answered, pushing my way past her and into the room. But the bed wasn't empty like I'd expected it to be. A man with a missing ear, wounded legs and bloodstained bandages lay unconscious on the mattress. It made my stomach churn to think I must have looked ten times worse than this when I hit the pavement. I thought about the moment I jumped. I remembered that I looked into Sunday's eyes as I fell and saw them gleaming helplessly as I plummeted to the ground. I recalled that the look in his eyes confused me because we didn't know each other, yet he seemed so sad that I was going to die. Probably only because they needed me to win this war. Well, that's what I'd thought until Storm told me I was virtually useless.

"Ember."
Someone rested a hand on my shoulder. I looked into Aster's face and asked, "What happened to him?"
"He accidentally activated a Block when he was on his way back to Peak after patrolling the Outside," she told me. I looked at the man and thought of my brother. I didn't remember him well, but I was frightened by what they might

be doing to him over in Three. If those people could create the Blocks and Snappers, what else were they capable of? Anything. That was the answer.

Chapter 13

"So, where am I meant to go?" I asked Aster once I'd had enough of looking at the poor man.
"You need to go to your bedroom. It's room 407," Aster answered. "We need this bed for other patients Ember. You're not in mint condition, I'll give you that, but there are people who are in much worse condition than you," she pointed at the bloody man. I nodded, agreeing that this man deserved a place in the hospital more than I did.
"Okay, but I have no idea where room 407 is," I said.
"Alora will take you. Speaking of Alora, where is she? I haven't seen her since she whisked you away for that meeting."
So, I told Aster about Zale refusing to rescue Theo, and how I'd stormed out. Aster gave me a friendly rub on the shoulder and told me Theo would be fine, nobody would have the heart to do anything horrible to a five-year-old.
"Don't worry I'm sure they'll rescue him soon. Now off you go, I have patients to tend to."
"Alright. Goodnight," I bid her. I left the room and stepped out into the reception, glad to be out of the small hospital room with the body of the man lying lifeless on the bed.

It had been a long day for me. Wanting to just climb into a bed and fall asleep, I began to make my way up the stairs,

planning to just wander around until I found room 407. It felt like an age before I reached the top of the third flight of stairs and a boy around my age approached me. "Ember!" said the boy, "It's good to see you out of the hospital at long last!"
"Yeah, I guess," I said, wondering who he was.
"I heard that you were out of bed and I have been looking for you ever since. Where have you been all day?" he asked brightly.
"Well, Alora took me to a meeting this afternoon and that's it," I replied as we made our way further up the stairs.
"Cool. Speaking of Alora, she said that you'd lost your memory, is it true?" he asked. Unsure whether or not to trust him, I just nodded and kept walking. "Do you remember me," he questioned.
"I don't really think so. But I could swear you're Ziggy or something like that, right?" I answered.
"Close. I'm Zandar or Zan, either's fine," he laughed.
"Right. Anyway, where have you been all day? If you'd been looking for me, surely I would have seen you around. I'd have thought you'd be at the meeting as well, but you weren't," I said.
"Oh, I couldn't make it to the meeting. I was...helping down in the engine rooms. The generator broke. Yeah, I was down there fixing it."
"Right, of course," I said, but I didn't believe him. I seemed to have caught him out because he'd stuttered when I asked him, and his smile was a little too wide. I gave him a suspicious glance and matched my pace to his.
"So, what did you talk about at the meeting?" he asked, obviously changing the subject. I decided not to tell him the whole truth but let him in on the general gist of what we'd talked about. I mostly ranted about Zale's refusal to rescue my brother. It felt good to let all my emotions pour out over someone, but it was clear Zandar wasn't listening.
"What's wrong?" I asked.

"Nothing," he replied vaguely. "Did you say that the army is going to break into Three?"
"Yes, why?" I asked.
"Oh, no reason. I just have fuzzy hearing and couldn't tell what you said," he replied, a little too quickly. Nice cover, Mr Shady I thought to myself. Zandar checked the watch on his wrist and said that he must go and sped off down the stairwell. "Our room is only on the next floor by the way!" he yelled up at me before disappearing. I walked up the rest of the stairs to our room, wondering why he was acting so strange.

I finally reached room 407 and pushed open the door. I walked in to find Alora getting changed into a robe. "There you are," she said, sounding relieved, "I wondered where you'd gone after you stormed out of the Cabin. By the way, have you seen Zandar today?" She sounded worried.
"Yeah, he just walked me up the stairs and then ran off. Why? Have you not seen him today?"
"Not since I got up this morning. He ran off and I haven't heard from him."
"He told me that the generator broke and he'd been fixing it and also that he'd been going around looking for me all day," I told her, pulling on a robe and slipping under the covers.
"Oh. He'd normally tell me what he was up to." Alora sounded hurt.
"Well, he was acting a little strange," I said.
"Never mind. He's always a little crazy. Maybe he didn't sleep well last night and so forgot to let me know. Let's just go to bed. Goodnight, Ember."
"Night," I replied. She turned out the light and I was left to think about Zandar's strange behaviour and where he'd run off to.

Chapter 14

When I woke up the next morning, the clock read 10:00. I yawned, stretched, and rolled over to find Alora's bed was empty. I sat up and found she was not in the living room either. Great, I thought. Now I'm all alone with nothing to do and I don't remember anything! Then I remembered my plan to get myself a weapon. I hopped out of bed, quickly washed in the small bathroom off to the side of the living room and got dressed. Then, I put up my hair and left. I started off down the stairs. It took a while to plod down to the Training Centre on the ninth floor using my robot shuffle, but I was determined. When I reached my destination, I found a maze of rooms, each one the size of a hall. I wandered around for ages, poking my head around doors in search of a weapon. But instead of weapons, I found multiple gyms, rooms filled with obstacle courses, rooms to practice archery, knot tying, camouflage and a million other things. Some rooms I avoided entering because through the doors I could hear orders being shouted and feet pounding the floor, as soldiers trained within. After hours of exploring all the rooms, I stumbled across the largest room of all. It was filled from floor to ceiling, every conceivable space, with weapons. Guns, crossbows, bows and arrows, swords, daggers and a hundred other deadly things.

I looked over my shoulder to make sure no one had followed me and crept inside the room. I was scared to move, certain that if I did I would accidentally set off one of the guns. I had no idea what weapon to choose because I didn't know what would be most helpful in the upcoming situation. Besides, I'd never used any of them in my life! Well, not unless the plastic bow and arrows I got one long ago Christmas counted. I was going to have to test the guns and crossbows to see which was the best. I first went and picked up the smallest bow. It was a good weight and fairly easy to carry. I loaded it with an arrow and aimed for the only empty spot on the wall. I missed it by miles, so I had another try and got a tiny bit closer. I collected the arrows I'd launched and put them back in their sheath thinking I'd have no time to miss my target in a life-threatening situation.

I next tried out the crossbows and wasn't too far off my mark on the wall, but far enough to spare the life of an enemy. I finally picked up a small handgun. It looked pathetic next to all the others that were the same height as me. I'd never even wanted to touch a gun. Just the thought that they could kill someone in a second with the twitch of a finger scared me. Nobody should have that kind of power. Nevertheless, this was the easiest of the three weapons to hold so far. I focused on the same spot, wondering if I'd shoot through the wall with the bullets, took a deep breath and fired. As I pulled the trigger, the door opened. I panicked and my hands jerked. The bullet ricocheted off the blade of a huge knife that was mounted on the wall. The knife spun off the wall towards the door. I closed my eyes, not wanting to see who I'd unintentionally killed but there was no cry of pain. I looked up to see Sunday. He was holding the knife in one hand and smirking. "Nice aim, sweetheart," he said. He threw the knife, and the tip of the blade hit the exact spot I'd been aiming for the whole time. Then he smiled and strolled off.

Muttering in irritation, I left the armoury with the gun and walked back down the corridor trying to look as innocent as possible. I made my way back up to my room. When I opened the door, I found Alora and Zandar sitting on the sofa sharing a bowl of what seemed to be blue Doritos. Suddenly, I was dying for crisps. Any kind. It had been at least five months since I'd had any. "Hey, Ember," said Alora.
"Hi," I said, shuffling over to my bed, with the gun hidden behind my back.
"Where have you been all morning? I haven't seen you," asked Zandar.
"I could say the same for you," I countered, "You ran off last night and weren't here this morning." Zandar stuttered as he tried to think up a lie to answer my question.
"He was probably working on the generator again, weren't you, Zan?" Alora cut in.
Zandar, looking relieved for the help, said; "Yeah, I was. It keeps breaking down." I knew this was a lie, but I nodded and slipped the gun under my bed clothes.
"You like crisps, Ember?" Alora asked me, changing the subject.
"I love them," I replied, walking to the sofa and sitting down with them.
"Here," Zandar handed me one of the blue Doritos. I crunched down on it and found it delicious. Realising I hadn't eaten breakfast and it was half eleven in the morning, I stuffed more of the crisps into my mouth and asked, "Will we have lunch soon?"
"Yeah. We'll go to the diner, they've got fish and potato on the menu today," Alora told me.
"You must be hungry, we didn't see you at breakfast this morning," said Zandar, still hinting that he wanted to know where I had been.

I just nodded and said, "Yeah, I'm starving. So, where's the diner? I don't remember going there before."
"No, you haven't, you've only ever eaten in the Cabin. The diner's on the third floor, it's where they make all the food," said Alora.
"Do we only get small portions because of the rationing?" I asked.
"I'm surprised you remember that, seeing as we told you about it before you jumped. But yeah, the portions are fairly small" said Zandar. I nodded, then Alora told us that if we wanted to be first in the lunch queue then we should probably make our way down now. So we all got up and they led me down to the third floor for lunch.

Chapter 15

When we arrived at the diner, I was shocked. Everything I'd seen of One was perfect, sparkling white, with a splash of emerald green here and there. The diner, however, was a whole other story. The walls were painted hot pink and the tiles on the floor were chequered white and the same shade of pink. All the booths were striped red and white, like the ones you see in old American sitcoms. There was a bar, a counter where food was served, and cakes displayed in glass cases. It was like a replica of a retro diner. It was the closest thing to normal I'd seen since I'd been down here.

"How come it's so colourful here?" I asked as we took plates and walked to the counter.
"Well, the person who runs the diner, Dolly, loves pink and bright colours and all that stuff. Plus, she wanted to replicate a real American diner from the Above," Alora said.
"Well, she did a pretty good job," I said as a friendly looking old woman ladled fish pie onto my plate.
"Hey, Dolly," Zandar said to the woman.
"Hey there, Zan," she replied. She turned to me and said, "And you must be the girl that fell down from the Above and jumped from Peak to try and save her brother." I nodded. "Aren't you a shrinking violet!" she then said, and I smiled.

The three of us went and found a booth to sit at and dug into our fish pie. "Are there any oceans down here?" I asked.
"No," answered Alora.
"So, where'd this fish come from?"
"It's man made. The only oceans down here are oceans of old sewer water," answered Zandar. Alora and I grimaced. After a moment of silence Sunday came in, took a tray and a plate, and walked up to the counter. He and Dolly exchanged a friendly conversation and then he brought his tray over and sat down next to me on the booth. This was awkward. I wondered if he'd tell them about earlier when I almost killed him with that flying knife but, thankfully, he didn't. Instead, he asked the two of them; "What do you guys have next?" This question triggered long forgotten memories of my school life to flood my mind. I thought of all my friends, the teachers, and lessons I hated. The summer holidays would have come and gone, and all my friends would have moved up into year 11 without me. That life all seemed like a dream. Like it had never really happened. Alora groaned which forced my mind back to the diner and my fish pie which was slowly growing cold. "We've got to go and help Pluto in the labs. She needs us to teach her team how to build bomb shells." I took a mouthful of fish pie and wondered what I'd do after I'd finished eating.
"I'd rather do that than more training. It's like I haven't left the gym since Zale started planning the break-in," said Sunday, grumpily.
"It's tomorrow that you're putting your plan into action, right?" asked Zandar.
"Yeah. I'd better be going. Come to think of it, Zale will lose it if he knows I've been 'wasting' time chatting with you guys. See you later." Sunday stood up, put his plate in a large sink and left, heading for the Training Centre.
"Do you know what time they're leaving tomorrow?" I asked Alora and Zandar.

"Umm, I think they're going very early. Zale said about five in the morning, why?" Alora replied.
"Oh, no reason, just wondered," I told them.

By the time the three of us had finished eating, the whole diner was bustling with people on their lunch break. I recognised some of them. I saw Neptune who smiled at me, and Ruben and Riggs passed by our booth. Alora and Zandar went off to the labs and left me to puzzle over what I should do. I wondered if there was anything I could do to prepare for tomorrow's early start. I had a gun for defence and the map of Three, so I'd have a vague idea of where to go when we arrived. All that was left to do was find out where the army was leaving from tomorrow morning and to find out where Theo was being held prisoner.

I made my way back up to the ninth floor, my muscles feeling stronger all the time, in hope of overhearing a conversation which would help me find out where to go in the morning. It appeared that luck was in my favour. After hearing hushed voices and footsteps, I dived into the nearest room and managed to conceal myself under a cargo net just in time, as Zale and Sunday entered after me.
"Five o'clock, right?" Sunday asked.
"Yes, five o'clock. Right here. We'll gather in this spot before we leave," Zale replied.
Sunday nodded then said; "Oh and Zale....actually never mind."
"Spit it out Sunday, I haven't got all day!" Zale shouted. Geez, he's got a very short temper, I thought. "Well, I was just wondering... are you sure we can't at least try to get Ember's brother? We wouldn't need the whole squad, of course, just one or two of us. I could go if that's alright with you," Sunday questioned. I felt a pang of hope in my heart. Maybe, just

maybe, Zale would agree. That way I wouldn't have to make the perilous mission to Three.

"Sunday!" Zale was right in Sunday's face, "How many times will I have to refuse this rescue mission? I've said no to Ember enough as it is, and I will not have you begging me to save an unimportant little five-year-old! No harm will be done if he's left to die! They can't use him in Three for anything anyway, he's probably dead already!" Zale spat. The small flicker of hope in my heart was extinguished and replaced with a flame of anger.

"Zale, come on! Have a heart! We both know that we could save him, you just won't!" Sunday shouted.

"Sunday, I am the commanding officer, I make the rules, it's my job. Do you know what your job is? Your job is to follow those rules! I will not risk the lives of my men by sending them down into the labs just to rescue a boy who is as good as dead and completely and utterly disposable, alive or not! Get back to training!" Zale stormed out leaving Sunday standing alone. It was all I could do not to jump out of my hiding spot and shake Zale. Theo was not disposable or unimportant. And I was going to make sure that he was rescued.

After Sunday had left the room, I crept out from my hiding spot and made my way back to room 407. I set an alarm on my clock for 4:30am the next morning. It would give me twenty minutes to get ready and ten minutes to hide myself under the cargo net again before the army gathered. I began preparing everything I would need - a fresh pair of clothes, the map, and the gun. Everything was running smoothly. It had only been about two hours since I'd had my fish pie in the diner, but I went into the kitchen in search of something to eat anyway. I planned to go to bed extra early, so I'd have enough energy for tomorrow. There wasn't much in the fridge except for a block of pink cheese, a few slices of purple ham and a tiny bit of green pasta.

It took me a while to get to grips with the gas hob but eventually I had a small bowl of ham and cheese pasta. Feeling proud, I went and sat on the sofa and ate my tiny dinner, hoping that nobody would come in and bother me. Thankfully, I was left alone and once I'd finished eating, I changed into the white robe hanging on the bedpost and crawled under the covers.

I couldn't tell how long it had been, half an hour, an hour, maybe, when the door creaked open, and Alora and Zandar came in. "Oh! There she is!" Alora sighed in relief.
"I told you she'd be here," said Zandar. "It's a bit early for bed, isn't it?"
"She's not fully recovered from her fall yet, Zan. She was probably feeling lightheaded. Be quiet though, she might be asleep," Alora replied. They both tiptoed over to the sofa and sat down. I tossed and turned in bed but couldn't get to sleep. Their conversation about what they'd had for dinner wasn't helping me drop off.

Chapter 16

I had no idea what time I'd gone to sleep but it was much later than I'd planned. I had no time to worry about how much sleep I had gotten though. The alarm I'd set last night had buzzed under my pillow until it woke me up. I hurried into the bathroom as silently as I could and had a quick shower and brushed my teeth. As I was getting dressed, I wondered where all the clean water down here came from but there was no time to waste thinking about that now. I zipped the gun up in my jacket pocket, folded up the map and slipped it into my other pocket. Lastly, I wrote a note to Alora telling her I'd gone to Three and slipped the pen in with the map.

Ten minutes to go.

I then dashed into the kitchen and had a breakfast of the blue Doritos and a glass of water.

Seven minutes.

I sped out of the room and flew down the stairs, stumbling on every other step.

Three minutes.

I reached the ninth floor and hurtled through the maze of corridors until I reached the room that the army would be meeting in.

One minute left.

I could already hear the marching footsteps of the men as I closed the door behind me.

Thirty seconds.

I dived behind the cargo net, my heart pounding. I could finally spare a second to breathe again. The door swung open, and Zale led the troop of men inside. They stood in a perfectly straight line. Zale paced up and down the line of his soldiers, inspecting their uniform. I spotted Sunday in the line and hoped he hadn't seen me. "Right men! It is exactly five o'clock, but you know my motto! Five minutes early is too late. I expect better next time," Zale hollered in his scratchy voice. "Now, get your weapons and assemble back in the line." As Zale said this he pointed at the cargo net. Terrified, I froze, as the men began making their way over to the net in an orderly line. SUGAR! I thought. All the weapons the army would be taking to Three had been arranged against the net, right in front of my face. In my panic to hide I hadn't noticed that they were there. I had to find somewhere else to hide. There was a climbing wall next to the net. I quickly crawled on my hands and knees and hid behind the wall just as the first person picked up a gun.

All the men took a weapon and finally the last one re-joined the end of the line. "Excellent soldiers. Now, I trust you don't need me to go over the plans again? Good, then let's go," Zale said. From my hiding space behind the climbing wall, I couldn't see what was going on, but I could hear them leaving. I waited until the last man had left and crept out. I crossed to the door and twisted the handle.

The door was locked. I swore under my breath and searched frantically for a key or something to pick the lock with, but I found no such thing. I kicked the door in a storm of rage and slumped against a wall. Then a thought crossed my mind as my eyes fell on a sheath of arrows. I could try and use an arrow to unlock the door. I yanked an arrow out of the sheath and jiggled it around inside the lock. It seemed that again, luck was in my favour.

The door swung open and I dashed out and listened for the sound of rhythmic footsteps. There! I could hear them! I ran towards the sound and just glimpsed the last person turning the corner ahead. I slowed down a bit, not wishing to be seen or heard and followed a safe distance behind them. We walked and walked and walked. After a while I began to daydream and wonder what path we would be taking to Three. We'd passed through a huge white door that I'd never seen before and now I found myself walking through a narrow concrete passage with no windows. The walls seemed to be closing in on me when Zale's harsh voice brought me back to reality. The man in front of me stopped so abruptly I had almost walked straight into him. "Alright, men! On the other side of this door is The Portal. Once I open the door there is no turning back, do you understand?" There was a murmur of agreement from the squad. "Here's to all of you who don't make it back!" Zale saluted and the squad saluted back. The door opened and Zale was gone. The men began their march again and disappeared straight through The Portal. I felt caught off guard. I hadn't expected anyone to die on this mission. But what was I thinking? This was war, of course there would be deaths. Maybe in the next few minutes. Maybe one of them would be my own.

Chapter 17

I was the last to make it through The Portal of course. I had not given much thought to not blowing my cover once we'd left One and there was no time to think about it now. As soon as I'd passed through The Portal I was standing in the exact spot where me and Theo had almost been devoured by the Snapper so long ago. "Ember?" said Sunday. The whole squad was staring at me.

"Hi." I gave an awkward smile.

Zale was speechless. He spluttered, "What!?" clearly fuming.

I replied "I've come to rescue my brother. I knew you weren't going to. I will not leave him to die as some people wish me to. Don't bother trying to make me go back, I'm not going."

Zale shook his head. "We don't have time for this! You're risking your life by doing this kid, but I know I'm not going to change your mind. God, I'm going to be arrested for letting you come with us! Let's go men!" Zale shouted.

The men began to jog, staying close to the slimy dank walls. They had guns and crossbows at the ready, so I decided to pull out my gun to protect myself. Sunday stopped jogging and slowed down so I could catch up with him. "You don't know what you've gotten yourself into," he whispered in my ear.

"I don't care. I just want to save Theo," I replied, dismissively. Sunday shook his head and resumed jogging. After a while, I slipped off into my own world and let my feet carry me onwards.

It was weird to think that we were inside a massive sewage pipe, and I still couldn't get my head around the fact that people actually lived down here. Right beneath our feet. "Stop!" Zale hissed, dragging me away from my thoughts. There was an urgency in his voice, and he signalled for us to crouch. He then shone a torch into the never-ending gloom up ahead. There was nothing there and he signalled for us to continue. We crept ahead, our backs pressed against the slimy pipe.

That's when we heard it.

A shriek.

An ear-piercing shriek.

A shriek that made our blood run cold and our hearts skip a beat.

I froze and Sunday thrust his arm out in front of me, as if to protect me. I could hear my own heart pounding in terror. Every crossbow was loaded, every gun was cocked. Zale shone the torch beam into the gloom again and we saw a troop of Snappers charging towards us. The soldiers moved into position and prepared to shoot the Snappers.

Chapter 18

The first Snapper leapt and closed his jaws around a soldier's neck, only to be shot by another soldier. "Pete!" someone cried. That's when everything went crazy. Shrieks and gunshots echoed down the pipe and into the darkness. Bullets and arrows flew through the air, jaws snapped, and tails swiped. Soldiers cried out in pain and Snappers screamed with their dying breath. There were people and Snappers dropping dead all around me. Black ooze gushed from the Snapper's bullet and arrow wounds. Blood poured from the bite marks on the soldier's necks and chests. The stream of sewer water mingled with the blood and black ooze and formed a foul sticky substance. I held back, crouching low and fired a couple of shots with my gun, but missed every time.

It feels like hours before all the Snappers were finally dead. The smell of blood and slime polluted the air, making me feel sick. I stood in silence and looked around at the graveyard of men and alligators. I tried to take a few deep breaths to settle my stomach, but it only made things worse and I ended up vomiting all over myself. Great, I thought. Now I'm covered in vomit as well as sewer water and blood.
"Speak up if you're alive!" I heard Zale call. It was so quiet. I was beginning to think I was the only one left alive. I made a

small noise, but nobody heard me. Suddenly, gentle arms were wrapped around my shoulders.

"You alright?" Sunday asked.

"Yeah, I managed to hide," I replied, thinking how cowardly I must sound.

"Good. There's not many of us left. Although you are hopeless at combat, you're better than nothing," Sunday said, his voice hoarse with pain.

I was about to ask if he was alright, when Zale hollered angrily; "Enough of the chit-chat, you two!"

"You okay?" I asked Sunday, completely ignoring Zale.

"Well..." Sunday pointed down to an enormous Snapper tooth that had impaled him in his gut. I gasped, feeling pathetic that I was the one who had been asked if I were alright.

"We need to pull that out," Zale said, approaching us.

"Will he die?" I asked Zale.

"Shouldn't do. I'll be honest though, you really need a surgeon."

"Great. Can't you just pull it out and get this over with?" Sunday asked impatiently.

"I can try" Zale called out someone's name, who replied weakly and tried to sit themselves up. Zale rushed over to them, helped them up and took a large bandage from their pocket. Other than myself, Zale and Sunday, there appear to be only fifteen or so survivors.

Zale came back and propped Sunday up against one of the slimy walls. He sat there struggling to breathe and trying to suppress groans of pain. I crouched next to him, trying to avoid the streams of blood. Zale pressed his right hand around the wound and used his left to pull out the tooth. Sunday only made a small cry of pain before fainting. Seeming unconcerned that Sunday was unconscious, Zale wrapped the bandage tightly around Sunday's gut. He then called Sunday's name, shook his shoulders, pinched him hard and rubbed his chest with his knuckles. I remember learning that this was the way you were supposed to wake somebody that was unconscious. It worked and Sunday opened his eyes. Zale told me to make sure he was alright and went to help the other injured men.

Sunday gave me a weak smile and looked deep into my eyes. He pulled a face which suggested he was thinking deeply and then had a lightbulb moment. Taking a piece of cord from around his neck, he wiped the tooth on his shirt and tied the cord around it. "Here. A necklace for you." I slipped it over my head. "That cord is my lucky charm. My mother gave it to me before she passed away. So now you have my luck. I could swear animal teeth are meant to be lucky too."
"Thanks," I said, marvelling at the weight of the tooth around my neck.
"Don't mention it." As we sat in silence, I realised I could feel his breath on my cheeks and count all the tiny scars that were scattered across his face. I did not know what to say or do. I froze like I had when I had heard the Snappers running down the tunnel. I could swear that he was inching slowly closer to me. Before I knew what was happening, our lips were locked together. My eyes widened in shock and my heart started to pound. After a moment I closed my eyes, enjoying the feeling.
"Is he alright?" Zale called down to me. I pulled away and answered with a feeble "yes".

That hadn't been the right time to kiss me. I'd just vomited and stank of blood and ooze. Sunday was probably disgusted. Trying to make it less awkward between us, and failing, I asked him how he was feeling. I couldn't quite look him in the eye anymore. That wasn't to say I didn't like the kiss, but I just didn't think it was the right place or time. "I'm not so bad.

A little sore," Sunday said, prising me away from my thoughts.
"That's good. But you're not going to have any time to recover, Zale is clearly getting impatient." I pulled him up off the floor and we waded over to Zale and the other survivors.

After everyone had said their goodbyes to the dead, those of us remaining made our way down the tunnel. "Right men," Zale said as we began to wade, "I think that's all the Snappers dead. We've just got to look out for water snakes and Blocks now. Don't let your guard down." Nobody spoke after that, so I was left to my own thoughts.

We trudged for ages through the dank water. All I could think about was the kiss. I tried to push it from my mind without success. Sunday came over to talk to me a few times, but I flushed a deep shade of red whenever he did, so after a while he gave up.

After perhaps an hour of wading through the filth, we reached a Portal. It was identical to The Portal that was the entrance to One, except for the fact that it was swirling shades of blue instead of purple. "This is the entrance to Two," Zale announced for my benefit, as the others surely knew this. Once we had passed The Portal it became much harder to walk, as the stream of sewer water had risen to my stomach. Any deeper, and I was going to have to swim. Just the thought of swimming in this made vomit rise in my throat again. To make matters worse, we could only see by the light of Zale's torch. The flickering, dim lamps hanging from the roof of the tunnel, had burned out about two miles ago.
"Couldn't we have brought a boat, or a canoe or something!" I said.

"At the moment that would be useful," a soldier replied, "But it's only going to get deeper and the current stronger. It would be too hard to control."

By the time we'd reached the third portal, I had to swim. Most of the squad had to do the same. I looked up at The Portal, eager to go through and get out of this revolting water. This time, The Portal was different shades of churning green that put me in mind of witches making potions in cauldrons. "In we go!" cried Zale.

Chapter 19

The soldiers began climbing into The Portal, and I was boosted in. I felt a strange sucking sensation as I passed through. Thankfully, I was one of the first to go through. Once on the other side, I found myself in a cold dark hallway. It was lit by the same flickering lamps that illuminate parts of The Outside. Flashes of green also lit the hall as the rest of the men came through. I shook myself off like a dog, which did virtually nothing to make me dryer. Zale checked all the guns and crossbows to make sure they still worked after getting wet. He then pulled out a device which scanned ahead for any dangers, and we crept down the hall. “I don’t know whether they’re expecting us, so be ready for battle,” Zale told us as we approached a door at the end of the hall that led into the city.

Chapter 20

I was surprised to find that it was night-time when we entered the city. It was the crack of dawn when we'd left One. Had we really spent that long in the tunnel, or was their Dome set to a different time? A cool breeze blew through my hair which again surprised me because we were underground. Streetlamps were illuminating the cobblestones beneath our feet, so at least I could see where I was going. I looked around to find a totally different world compared to One. Everything was imperfect. Uneven cobblestones, sloping roofs on the log cabins that the citizens must live in, crooked iron fences. I had to admit, this place was kind of cosy and quaint. All the houses formed winding roads with small front gardens. There were shops and restaurants, and I was certain I could see a theatre off in the distance. "How come it's so much nicer here than in One?" I asked Zale.

"One is a place of business and command. We're the city with the power. It was built for efficiency," he replied, "But there's no time for pointless questions such as these. We must be getting to work! Split into groups. You'll need one medic with each group and one leader. Go!" Everyone split into groups of four. They did it so seamlessly, like well-oiled clockwork. By the time they'd finished it was just me left standing awkwardly on my own. "You're still going after your brother, aren't you?" asked Zale. He sighed when I nodded defiantly and continued; "Alright, but you can't go alone. Sunday, you take her, you know the way. He'll be in the labs. Now everyone, once your jobs are completed assemble back here. Do not leave until everyone is back." With that everyone ran off in different directions leaving me and Sunday alone.

We jogged at a steady pace for about half a mile and then we reached a large manhole. "We're going down there, aren't we?" I asked, already knowing the answer. As I expected, Sunday pulled off the cover. Then we both jumped down and found ourselves in another long hallway. We picked back up with our jogging. We didn't speak or make eye contact the whole way down the hall. I heard Zale a few times in Sunday's earpiece, but I couldn't make out what he was saying and I wasn't going to ask.
"Stop!" Sunday whispered as we reached the door at the end of the hall. We both stood either side of the door and waited, for what, I could only guess.

I heard distant voices and before I knew it, somebody had kicked open the door and it flew back, slamming into my face. I slid down the wall, blood gushing from my nose as two armed soldiers began shooting at Sunday. He put up a good fight, bullet shells flying everywhere. I wiped the blood from my nose and stood up. Until now, the two soldiers hadn't noticed me because I'd been hidden by the door. One of them turned to me and pulled the trigger on his gun. It appeared to be my lucky day because he was out of bullets, but this didn't faze him. He threw his gun to the floor and advanced on me. Behind him, I saw Sunday and the enemy soldier had discarded their guns too and were engaged in hand-to-hand combat.

The soldier put his hands tightly around my neck and held me a few inches off the ground. I started to panic but forced myself to calm down knowing it wouldn't help. I brought up my legs and use them to kick him. Then, seeing his gun on the floor, I remembered I had my own. I slipped my hand into my jacket pocket, pulled out the gun and shot him in the stomach. He immediately doubled over and fell to the floor. It was mere seconds before his eyes glazed over and he lay limp on the stone beneath my feet. I gasped and put my hands over my mouth. I'd just killed someone. An innocent man. Yes, he was trying to kill me but even so! I was fifteen years old and I'd just shot someone dead.

The next thing I knew, Sunday was pushing me through the door. "Ember," he said, "If you're going to have a breakdown every time you shoot someone, you may as well stay here."
"I won't. But forgive me for feeling like a murderer. Well, I am, after all I've just killed someone!" I whispered back. He just shook his head, and we kept walking.
We moved further and further underground, down endless flights of stairs. The temperature dropped drastically. It felt like we wouldn't stop descending until we'd reached the very centre of the Earth.

Long after I'd lost count of how many flights of stairs we'd gone down, we reached a white door. I shot the lock with my gun and the door swung open and we both slipped through. About ten people in long white lab coats were surrounding a table, all facing us with shocked expressions. I studied each of their faces in turn as everyone seemed frozen in surprise. One particular face caused me and Sunday to double take. We knew one of the people in the white coats.

It was Zandar.

I had no time to puzzle over this, however, because the scientists had pulled themselves together and were charging at us with syringes and scalpels. Without thinking, I shot four of them point-blank before I ran out of bullets. They fell to the floor as blood stains blossomed on their white coats. This time I couldn't think about what I'd done because there were two more scientists charging at me. I threw the gun at one of their heads, and he stopped running to clutch the wound. And I ran. I ran out of the windowless, white lab which reminded me so much of One. I sped through a side door, a man with a syringe hot on my heels. Through the side door was another room, much the same as the one I'd just escaped from. The only difference was that on all four walls are large glass cells. I could see someone in a cell. Someone very familiar.

Theo.

Though my memory had been patchy before, seeing my little brother unlocked so many memories. I remembered my sisters and my parents. I remembered that secretly, Theo had always been my favourite. But there was no time to explore my newly rediscovered memories.

"Ember!" Theo mouthed. He must have been screaming, but the glass he was trapped behind was soundproof.
"Theo!" I ran up to the glass and pounded it with my fists. It achieved nothing. I kicked the glass. Still nothing. The last thing I remembered was Theo pointing over my shoulder and mouthing something.

Chapter 21

My eyes flickered open. Panic pulsed through me. Where was I? What was going on? My head was groggy and I found that it weighed a ton when I attempted sitting up. There was something sticking out of my shoulder. I pulled on it and out came a syringe. My mind flashed back to the last few moments that I remembered. The scientist with the syringe who now laid dead on the floor in front of me, must have stabbed me and injected something into my veins that made me pass out.

It seemed like I was always waking up with no idea what was going on. It happened so often, that it didn't even phase me anymore. This must be, what? The fourth time? Ignoring the splitting pain throbbing in my head. I stood up and advanced towards the dead scientist. I only made it a few steps before I found that I couldn't walk any further. Of course. Like Theo, I had also been imprisoned in a glass cell. In the opposite cell, I saw the silhouette of Sunday. He stood up and banged the glass, mouthing something unintelligible to me. Feeling like a caged animal, I also pounded the glass and shouted Sunday's name, but I knew he couldn't hear me. In the cell closest to me I saw Theo. Tears were streaming down his face as he looked at me, his eyes wide with fear. I threw the syringe at the glass and sank onto the small iron bed in the corner of my cell.

All I could think about was how bad I smelt. Wading and then swimming in old sewage hadn't done me any favours. My clothes were still a little damp and there were stains on my shirt and trousers that I couldn't even mention. I sat on my bed breathing in the toxic aroma and feeling sorrier for myself by the second.

At that moment someone walked in and approached my cell. It was Zandar. I remembered how strange he'd acted when I told him about the planned invasion of Three. Now I knew why. I banged the glass and yelled insults at him. He pushed a button on a gadget he was holding and suddenly I heard his voice bouncing off the glass of my cell. I looked around and could tell that Sunday and Theo heard him too. "Please calm down!" he said.
"Calm down?!" I yelled incredulously.
"Ember, Ember! Please!" he said. Knowing there was an endless stream of insults to throw at him and that I'd never have the time to say them all, I shut up. "Thank you," he looked relieved. "You must all be surprised to see me here," he said calmly. Now it was Sunday's turn to holler abuse and pound the glass. Hurt registered on Zandar's face. When Zandar had finally had enough, he pressed a button on the remote he was holding. Sunday instantly leapt back from the glass and writhed around on the floor while bolts of blue light flickered around him.
"No!" I shouted, "Zandar, you little-" I let out a stream of insults and almost shattered the glass in my rage. The next thing I knew, I was the one writhing around on the floor with the blue light frying me. It felt like a million electric shocks.
"Had enough now?" I heard Zandar say through the speaker. He sounded smug. It made a tight knot of fury tie itself up

inside of me. I gave a weak nod and laid on the floor as the tingling from the shocks ebbed away.

"Try anything else and that will be the consequences. Same goes for you, Theo." I looked over to my little brother and saw him start at the mention of his name. His face was red and blotchy from crying and his face was a mask of horror from watching me being stabbed with the syringe and then electrocuted. Both Sunday and I laid twitching on the floor as Zandar continued. "This was never supposed to happen. You were never meant to find out about me-"
I cut him off. "You can't keep us locked up in here and frazzle us with bolts of electricity!" Zandar just gave me a pitying look and tried to continue but I cut in again. "What are you going to do with us anyway?" I rose from the floor on shaky legs.
"Shut up, Ember!" Zandar shouted at me. We all had to cover our ears because he was shouting so loudly. I was tempted to keep interrupting him, just to get on his nerves but decided not to, knowing it would just result in another round of electric shocks. "Thank you," he sighed. "Now, I'm in charge of all the prisoners down in the labs. I've decided against letting you return home-"
"What! No! I'm going home! Zandar, don't be an idiot, where's the boy I've grown up with all my life?" Sunday remarked, a pleading tone in his voice.
"How could you? Are you saying that me and Theo are going to have to live the rest of our lives down here?" This got on his last nerve and me and Sunday found ourselves thrashing around on the floor again. Theo's wails echoed off the glass walls. We silenced ourselves and reluctantly listened to what he had to say.

Chapter 22

A bowl of overly milky porridge and a glass of water were slipped into my cell. I sat and ate in silence thinking about what Zandar had said next; "Anyway, there won't be a rest of your lives! I'm having you executed!"
I heard my own incredulous voice echo through my head; "Why? You have no reason to do that!"
"Oh yes I do," Zandar said to me. "Storm didn't tell you the whole prophecy that is written in 'The History of Lowerground'. The last paragraph says:

'Watch for the girl with fire inside of her, because she will be both the saviour and destroyer of Lowerground. When all have been defeated, she will sit upon a throne of skulls. She will rule, always and forever.'

I hadn't believed Zandar, so I asked; "If that's true, then why didn't it say that in Storm's copy of the same book? I read the last paragraph myself and it didn't say that!"
"Yes, I know. Storm did that on purpose. He tore off the bottom of the page," Zandar answered.
"But why?" I questioned.
"Because he thought if you didn't know that you were supposed to *'rule always and forever'* then you wouldn't be able to fulfil the prophecy and he could continue to rule."

"But I don't want to rule forever! I just want to get my brother and go home. That's what I've wanted from the very beginning. If you let us go home, I wouldn't be here to *rule forever!*"

"Enough! I'm tired of this! I don't want any more excuses!" Zandar yelled.

He then went on to say that we'd have to be executed because Three were going to rule Lowerground. I argued that if that were the case, only I should be murdered but his mind was made up. The three of us, Sunday, Theo and I, would be dead by noon tomorrow.

I returned from my thoughts of the conversation between Zandar and myself and finished the rest of my porridge. We needed to get out, but how? The Snapper tooth necklace was still hanging around my neck, but I didn't see how it would come in useful. I needed to communicate with Sunday but Zandar had disabled the intercom so we could no longer talk. I emptied my pockets in search of something, anything useful. All I found was the map of Three and a marker pen that I had written the message to Alora on. I thought back to writing the note. Who knew how long ago that was. One thing I could be sure of was that Zale and the rest of the army would have given up on us and returned to One by now. Then I suddenly realised! The marker pen! I could use it to write on the glass and get messages across to Sunday. I picked up the pen and prayed that swimming in the sewer water hadn't damaged it. Yes! It still worked! I had to write backwards so Sunday could read the message properly. I scrawled a message on the glass and had to wait for Sunday to look at my cell. I knew banging the glass wouldn't make a difference as he couldn't hear me. Eventually, he read the message and shrugged his shoulders, telling me he didn't know what to do either. Disheartened, I rubbed away the message, and we both sat in silence for hours thinking, thinking, thinking.

It was only after dinner that Sunday suddenly jumped up with 'idea' written all over his face. He pointed to the ceiling, and I furrowed my eyebrows to tell him that I didn't understand. He dipped his finger in the bowl of stew we'd been given for dinner and used the orange gravy to write the word 'vent' on the glass. "Oh!" I said, even though he couldn't hear me. There was a small vent on the ceiling, just big enough for me to squeeze through and not get stuck. This was all very well but how was I supposed to get up there? I wrote my question on the glass in ink and Sunday replied in gravy with 'chair?' I pushed the chair that was next to my bed up under the vent and stood on it. Even if I jumped, I wouldn't be able to reach it. I groaned in frustration. I slumped against the wall and tried to think logically. Even if we could pull this off, there was an around the clock guard system. The only time we were left unwatched was during the couple of minutes it took for the guards to swap shifts. It was a mere eighteen hours until my body lie limp and dead. We needed to hurry. I rubbed the messages I'd written off the glass before anyone other than Sunday could see and then against my will, drifted off to sleep, exhausted by my journey to Three, the horror of the battle with the Snappers and taking a life, torture at the hands of Zander and the overwhelming fear of our situation.

Chapter 23

When I woke the next day I looked around the room. I was still alive. They hadn't killed me yet. I sat on the rickety chair as I ate my supposed last meal. A slice of bread and butter. Sunday and Theo were awake too and they both sat eating the bread on their chairs. All of us were doing the same thing. Counting down the minutes until we no longer could.

Tick tock. The beat of my heart matched the sound of the ticking clock mounted on my cell wall.

Tick tock. Minutes passed. The knot of fury in my stomach had been replaced by a knot of fear so tight it was painful.

Tick tock. I looked at Sunday. He was looking at me, taking in every tiny detail of the last sight he'd ever see.

Tick tock. I looked at Theo. He was so frozen with fear you might have mistaken him for dead already. Maybe the guards would let him go. He was only five after all.

Tick tock. I finally accepted that I'd never see my mum, dad or sisters again. I'd never go home to Southampton.

Tick tock. I could take it no longer. The knot of fear had tied up every muscle in my body and, like Theo, I found I couldn't move. It was like an invisible rope has tied me to the chair.

Tick tock. Around ten minutes until I was dead, I guessed.

Tick tock. I shouldn't have slept last night. I should have been trying to reach that vent and get us all out.

Tick tock. I saw that Sunday had been tied up by the same ropes as me and Theo.

Tick tock. We all sat looking at one another in turn. Five minutes now. The guards would be changing shifts any second and Zandar would arrive, wielding whatever he was going to kill us with.

Tick tock. I couldn't believe I had trusted him.

Tick t- I heard a strange noise. A noise like rusty metal being dragged against stone. What?

I looked up towards the sound and found the vent cover had been tossed aside. "Ember!" someone hissed. I saw a vaguely familiar face.
"Neptune?" I said, astonished.
"Yes, no time for chit chat. Come on." She dangled a rope into my face. I stood on the chair and clutched the end. I looked to Sunday and saw he too had a rope. I looked to Theo and saw someone helping him. I looked at the guards. They'd just left the room for their shift change.
"How'd you know we were here?" I asked, shimmying up the rope.

"One of my gadgets picked up Sunday's earpiece because all our technology runs on the same frequency. So we came to save you-"
"STOP!" Zandar had entered the room holding three sharp needles. I was already through the vent by the time he hit a button on his pathetic little remote. I found myself in a large ventilation system. All the walls were metal and there were many routes that we could take to escape. I saw Sunday and another spy further down the passage. I looked for Theo, but he was not there.
"Theo!?" I called but there was no reply. Another spy emerged from another vent shaft. Neptune asked him where Theo was.
"I couldn't save him in time," he replied. I cried out in despair and tears streamed down my face. I shoved Neptune and the other spy out of the way and looked down through the vent to see Theo frozen in the act of stretching up his arms for help. His eyes blinked and his chest moved as he breathed but every other muscle in his body appeared unable to move. That's what Zandar's button had done, paralysed him somehow.

I was about to lower myself back down when Sunday grabbed my arms and pulled me away from the hole. I threw him off me and attempted to reach Theo again. This time Neptune dragged me away and slammed the vent cover back down. "NO!" I screamed, slapping her, trying to get her to let go. "They're going to kill him! They're going to kill him!" I sobbed. Again, I lunged for the shaft, refusing to let them drag me away from my brother. The spy that had tried to rescue Theo held me back. I slapped and kicked him until he let go.
"EMBER!" shouted Neptune. She shook my shoulders and cuffed my wrists with strong plastic handcuffs to stop my attack. "It's too late! We must go before we are caught!" She signalled something to the other spies, and they began

crawling down the tunnel. Sunday slung me over his shoulder so I couldn't attempt to go back for Theo and then followed Neptune and the others. I wondered why Zandar hadn’t already followed us up into the vents but realised our escape must have taken him by surprise, and it would take him some time to organise some soldiers. Surely it wouldn’t be long though.

Chapter 24

I screamed, sobbed, and begged for them to turn back but they wouldn't. It was useless. My head dangled down and bashed into Sunday's back while he kept a firm grasp on my legs. I'd never see Theo again. He was dead. He was gone. Forever.

"Stop!" Neptune whispered. "We're approaching a section where there are going to be Blocks. Betta, go to the left and scan the area for gas Blocks. Maynard, to the right and scan the area for explosives. The two spies crawled off and Neptune turned to me. "Ember, I'm going to release you. Stay calm. It will be a lot easier if you do." She loosened the plastic cuffs, and my arms were free to move once again. For a moment I was calm and then I took a swing and punched her in the face. She stumbled back and I turned around, shoved Sunday aside and crawled back down the tunnel as fast as I could, screaming Theo's name. I knew Sunday was hot on my heels, so I sped up.

"Stop!" someone yelled at me, I ignored them and carried on. Next thing I knew, Maynard had jumped in front of me, blocking my path. "Ember, there are Blocks around here! We have to be careful!"

"Move!" I yelled. Using all my strength, I threw him against the metal wall and before I knew it the whole tunnel had been re-decorated with blood, bone fragments and shredded flesh. I screamed in shock and covered my eyes, thinking that if I couldn't see the scene in front of me it wouldn't be real, and Maynard would still be blocking my path. "I'm sorry. I'm sorry. I'm sorry," I whispered over and over again. Neptune would never be able to forgive me. What had I done!?

"Ember, get back here!" cried Sunday. Shaking, I scrambled back to them. There were so many things I could say to them, should say to them, but I remained in stunned silence.

"EMBER! WHAT HAVE YOU DONE?" Neptune yelled at me.

"I-I..." I didn't know what to say. Sorry just didn't seem to cut it. I didn't turn around. Whilst I didn't want to look at Maynard's splattered remains, the looks on everyone's faces would be much worse. I heard a sigh and Neptune spoke again in a quivering voice. "Maynard, may your soul rest in peace. Now get a move on! We can't lose anyone else!"

We continued crawling for miles and miles until Betta, the spy that had rescued Sunday, stopped. "There's a gas Block, right up ahead," she said. She and Neptune put odd mouthpieces into their mouths. They connected to tubes that were attached to oxygen packs on their backs. Betta produced two more packs and told me and Sunday to put them on. Then, I found myself crawling again. Betta signalled to Neptune that the Block had activated and we were entering the cloud of poisonous gas. All was fine for a little while and then my cheeks started to prickle. Confused, I felt my face and looked at Sunday who seems to be experiencing the same thing. I saw Neptune and Betta exchange a worried glance and quicken their pace. Suddenly, all the muscles in my face loosened and I felt my exposed skin start to sag. I gasped in alarm and the mouthpiece, which was giving me a flow of clean air, fell from my mouth. Luckily, I didn't breath in any of the toxic fumes, but it was close. I fumbled for the tube, but my melting face was too much of a distraction.

I was running out of air and would have to inhale any second. Suddenly, the other three stopped crawling. I saw their faces were drooping too, Betta's in particular. "We have to get out!" slurred Neptune. She had to take out the mouthpiece to speak but quickly puts it back in. I finally managed to put mine back into my mouth too and sighed in relief. I could breathe once again.

Next thing we knew Betta had dropped onto her front. We shook her and shook her but could tell by her sagging face that there was no waking her.

Chapter 25

I'd never known Maynard or Betta, or even seen them at Peak before, but they must have been very close to Neptune. Once we'd crawled to safety and out of the gas, Neptune slumped against the wall. Me and Sunday collapsed opposite her and ripped off our oxygen packs. Tears rolled down Neptune's face, swollen from when I'd punched her earlier, and slack from the gas, as she mourned for Maynard and Betta. Wanting to give her some privacy, I crawled further down the vent system with Sunday following me. The two of us sat huddled together listening to Neptune's sobs echo down the metal tunnel.

I leant my head against the metal wall and sighed. I felt my face. It was still tingling and slightly saggy from the gas but seemed to be getting better. Out of nowhere, Sunday put his arm around my shoulders, and I allowed it because my teeth were chattering, and I needed someone to hug. Also, because I liked it, although I didn't say as much.

Feeling slightly less tense, I took a proper look at my surroundings. Up until now I hadn't had a chance to take in the vent system and let the events of the past hour sink in. It was cold now that I was sitting down and not moving. The cool metal walls sucked out any heat there was in my body. I thought back to when I'd heard Neptune tossing the vent cover aside and went over what had happened since then.

I had been rescued and then attacked everyone apart from Betta in my desperation to reach Theo. For a moment I sat there and let the tears fall. How could I have left him there? How could I have let him slip from my fingertips again? Sunday wiped the tears from my cheeks and told me Theo would be alright. I knew it was not true and he was just saying it to make me feel better, but I nodded anyway and went back to my thoughts.

After I'd stopped trying to tear them all apart, I had been cuffed and carried down the system. I had accidentally got Maynard killed by shoving him into the Block. I added him to the tally of people whose deaths I was responsible for. We'd then lost Betta to the toxic gas. It was only me, Sunday and Neptune left.

I resurfaced into reality and listened to Sunday's heartbeat while Neptune blew her nose. I didn't think I was claustrophobic, but being trapped in the narrow, imposing vent system made me reconsider. The walls seemed to be closing in and I was finding it hard to breathe. I wondered if the walls would just keep getting closer until I was crushed and bloody. This image brought Maynard back into my mind, but luckily Neptune came over to us, distracting me.

"Sorry I took so long," she croaked. I wanted to tell her there was no need to apologise and that I should be the one saying sorry because of Maynard, but I couldn't. I was not good at apologising. Neptune sniffed and pulled out something that looked a little like the controller we'd use on the PS4 back at home. It was a Communicator, with a little screen which showed us a map of the vent system. Judging by the map, we only had to crawl for a few more minutes and we would reach a vent cover which would open into another of Three's underground labs. I feared that we would encounter more scientists but there was no time for worrying. The shaft was our only way out. "Let's go. We need to get back to One as soon as possible." Neptune said. Sunday and I nodded, rose to our knees and started crawling.

Once we were at the vent cover and had checked the Communicator to make sure we were at the right place, Neptune removed the cover and poked her head down. "It should be safe," she told us, lifting her head back up. "It's another lab and there's only one person down there. Follow me." We slid through the opening one at a time and jumped to the ground. It was a relief to be out of the claustrophobic system. I saw someone sitting at a bench doing something with test tubes and chemicals. He was wearing headphones and didn't appear to notice us. Sunday stole up behind him and with one punch knocked the unsuspecting man out. "Nice job," said Neptune. She made for the door, and we followed her.

Once through the door, we were in a long windowless hallway ending in stairs. Thankfully and much to my surprise we didn't come across anyone as we made our way up towards ground level.

Chapter 26

We finally climbed up through a manhole cover and dived behind a bush in someone's front garden. It was scratchy and uncomfortable, but no one could see us. I took a deep breath in to try and relax a little, but I almost choked on my own pungent smell which I'd been trying to ignore. The pain and guilt I felt about leaving Theo churned inside of me, stirring up a huge vat of anger. But as Sunday reminded me, there was no time for any distractions. We had to get back to One.

Neptune pulled out the Communicator and found a message from Storm. She read it aloud. "Neptune, what is going on? You've been totally off the grid for the last three hours! Are the others safe? I need information, everyone at Peak is panicking! Have you got any further intel on our escapee and Sunday? Get back to me ASAP. Storm". Neptune quickly sent a reply filling him in on the essentials. "Time to go, but we can't show our faces. Everyone knows who you are, Ember. Everyone either wants you dead, or under their governments control. So we'll have to disguise ourselves. Any ideas?" Neptune said.

"I'm sure whoever lives in this house will have something we could use," Sunday suggested.

"Good thinking. Let's get to work." Neptune replied.

We broke the door down using a bench from the neighbouring front garden. When we got inside, we found a woman standing in a doorway, grasping a chair so tightly her knuckles were white. She threw the chair at us, but it hit the wall and smashed. She ran down the hall screaming but Sunday quickly caught up and knocked her out. We ventured further into the house and found a drawer full of makeup in the woman's bedroom and I applied it to all our faces, making all of us look slightly odd but unrecognisable. We then pulled on large fluffy coats from the woman's wardrobe to disguise our tell-tale One outfits and set out for the street.

It was surprisingly easy to navigate our way through the streets using the Communicator. We eventually found our way back to the long corridor that ended with The Portal.
"That was easy," I said when we reached The Portal.
"Too easy," Neptune replied uneasily.
"I agree. I think someone knows we're here. Let's just get out of here before we get caught," Sunday said. We were about to step through The Portal when the Communicator started to buzz. Neptune tapped in a code and worry flooded her face as she saw whatever was making the communicator buzz.
"What. What is it?" I asked.
"It doesn't matter. The sooner we get out the better. Let's go!" Neptune answered. Me and Sunday exchanged a concerned look before jumping through The Portal after Neptune and landing with a splash in the Outside.

Chapter 27

As soon as I hit the water, I was submerged. I kicked and floundered, panic surging through me. I tried to get my head above the water's surface, but the current was too strong and it bore me down, dragging me into its clutches. "Ember!" I heard a distorted voice say, "Where are you?" I kicked and splashed, hoping that someone would see. But no one came. I was running out of air. A few more seconds and I would be dead. The strong current tore at me. The fluffy coat I'd stolen pulled me down until I hit the cold slimy bottom of the tunnel. I thrashed about but it was no use. I cannot describe the feeling of drowning. The utter panic, struggling to hold my breath and the burning sensation as the dirty water inevitably entered my lungs was too much for me to fight. I felt my life slipping away. This is the end, I thought.

This was the end.

?

Chapter 28

I coughed and spluttered, choking on the liquid that had flooded my lungs. I could not breathe. I could not see. I could not understand what was going on. After my lungs had finished expelling all the water, a river of vomit erupted from my mouth. I heard someone gag and felt them wipe my chin. Next thing I knew, I was locked in a tight embrace. I vomited again, down the back of whoever was hugging me. Cold water enveloped me. There was a current, but it was not as strong as when I was drowning. This is a strange after-life, I thought to myself. "You're alive!" I heard a breathy voice say. "You had me scared to death, Ember!" They sounded quite angry at me. I spluttered and choked again.

"I'm alive?" I managed to cough out.

"Yes. I saved you." I recognised the voice and arms as Sunday's. The boy who I suspected I might be falling in love with. I returned the hug.

"Sorry about the puke," I said to him feebly.

"Don't worry. I'm filthy and soaked anyways. Come on. We have to get back to One." Still a little confused and very weak, I began to swim after Sunday. Up ahead I could see Neptune. She shouted something I couldn't quite hear. Something about a snake, I thought. Suddenly, Sunday grabbed me by the wrist and pulled me onto his back. He told me to hold on tight as he began to swim as fast as he can.

Out of nowhere, an ear-splitting sound erupted from down the tunnel. A flicker of fear sparked inside of me. Snappers. This time we didn't have a troop of soldiers or any weapons. We were totally defenceless. All we could do was swim away. Neptune screamed orders at Sunday and he quickly obeyed. I tried to slide off his back so he could swim faster but he held tight and told me to stay put. Annoyed, I grudgingly listened to him. "Water snakes!" Sunday yelled, in answer to something Neptune had said. Water snakes? I think. And then I remembered. It was not only Snappers that plagued Lowerground. Three had also created water snake mutations in their underground labs.
There was another scream from down the tunnel and then a powerful wave of water washed over my head as something huge slammed against the tunnel wall. I looked back and saw the most terrifying sight of my life, even more petrifying than a Snapper. Five king cobras that must have been one hundred metres long were speeding towards us. Each one had metre-long fangs and enormous black flickering tongues. Their huge, evil eyes sought out my weak, vulnerable body in the darkness. Sunday's grip on me weakened and I slid from his back. Adrenaline surged through me, but I knew it was futile to even attempt escaping these snakes. I stared at the five sets of fangs hurtling towards me. Dripping with venom. Hungry for blood.

Chapter 29

I was willing something, anything, to save us. Please. Anything. I was swimming blindly forward, my arms kept on powering, and wouldn't stop until I was safe or dead. I gave a terrified yell. Sunday shouted something back, but my ears were too full of water to hear. It didn't really matter though; all I had needed was to know that someone was near. I was at the back of the group. Sunday was a few strokes ahead of me and Neptune was quite a way in the distance. I was annoyed that she had abandoned us, but I guessed I would have done the same thing.

A loud explosion rang through my head and up ahead I saw a huge mushroom cloud blossoming. After that everything went crazy. The Block had set off a chain of explosions that rumbled down the tunnel. I felt the cold breath of a snake on the back of my neck and began to panic just as another explosion triggered a wave that sent me tumbling and flipping through the water. I could feel and hear still more explosions around me. When I opened my eyes a snake was mere centimetres from my face. I let out a scream and my heart stopped. I'm going to die! I thought. What a horrible way to go.

But blessedly, it was dead. I could see that a great chunk of scaly flesh had been torn from its head by the explosions. Someone grabbed hold of the back of my shirt and dragged me through of the water. "EMBER! GO! GET OUT OF HERE!" Sunday hollered at me. How many times would this boy save my life? I swam as fast as I could and didn't look back. I couldn't see Neptune anywhere. She must have been killed in the first explosion, I thought in horror.

"Sunday!" I screamed. I could not bear the thought of being alone to face the snakes.

"I'm right here Ember! Keep going!" he yelled back. I twisted my head around to find there was only one snake left. The other's must have been blown to pieces by the explosions. I could see their bodies floating like buoys on the surface of the water. "Hurry up!" I shouted at Sunday. "Four down, one to go!" But he didn't hurry up. He grimaced in pain and momentarily stopped. I didn't know what had hurt him, but it didn't matter. Deciding it was my turn to save his life, I grabbed him around the waist and pulled him onto my back.

"Ember! You'll end up getting us both killed! You don't have to be a hero! Let me go!" Sunday begged me.

"No! It's my fault that we got captured and put in the cages in the first place. You stop being the hero and let me save you!" I shouted back. I wouldn't let him go but my arms were growing steadily weaker from exhaustion. I looked back again to find that the remaining snake has stopped and was looking at its four dead nest mates in anger and confusion. I didn't think they would have feelings, I thought to myself.

Hell bent on getting vengeance, the final snake began to slither down the tunnel, its cold, black eyes fixed on me. It opened its mouth, showing me its deadly fangs and hissed. My feet could almost reach the bottom of the tunnel now. Good, soon I'd be able to run. In a few more strokes the water was only up to my knees. I stood up and yanked Sunday across my shoulders in a fireman's lift. He weighed an absolute ton, but I couldn't put him down. The snake would catch him and eat him for sure.

It was difficult to run when my feet were still in the water, but it was definitely easier than swimming. I was hoping against hope that one last explosion would finish the snake off but no such luck. It seemed that all my luck was used up. I could hear the last cobra hissing and slithering towards me, catching up, and quickly. I picked up my pace. I could not run any faster for fear of collapsing from exhaustion. The weight of Sunday on my back was killing me but I had to keep going. He tried to get down several times, but I wouldn't let him and after a while he gave up, knowing it was just slowing us down.

Chapter 30

I gasped for breath. "Ember, just keep running!" Sunday screamed in my ear. I did. But I was now having to dodge the bodies of our squad and the Snappers that were still festering where we had left them after the battle several days ago. I almost vomited when the smell of their rotting flesh hit me. I heard Sunday gag when the stench reached his nose too. I raced through the grisly minefield of long-dead alligators and people. I could have sworn some of their lifeless claws and fingers were reaching for my ankles. This gave me a final burst of speed as I thought of all the zombie movies me and my friends had watched together when my life was still normal.

I ran and ran and ran. I ran until my legs were numb and turned back to see how far away the snake was. I was shocked to see it had stopped and was slithering between the bodies littering the tunnel. I kept on running, but I was looking back, eager to know what the snake was up to. I saw it dive down, grab a Snapper between its jaws and swallow it whole. Disgusted, terrified and weary, I turned my head forward and didn't look back. I couldn't stomach the idea that the cobra was actually eating the dead bodies. "Ember!" Sunday whispered, not wanting to alert the cobra that were still there. "Yes?"

"Look! Up ahead, do you see?" he asked me.
"No. What am I meant to be looking at?"
"That golden flash. Strain your eyes. Do you see it now?"
"Oh, yes. It's The Portal!" Overjoyed that we were almost there, I gave a loud whoop. Sunday clapped his hand over my mouth as I realised what I had done. The cobra raised its frilled head and hissed. "RUN!" Sunday yelled.
"I am!"
"Well go faster! Come on, we're almost there!" Using the last drop of energy I had, I bolted in the direction of The Portal. Almost there.

Almost.

Chapter 31

"Come on, just a few more steps!" It was a miracle that both of us were still alive. We should have been eaten by now. Or at least blown to pieces by the explosions. The cobra hissed from behind me. I felt its tongue rake my ankle. It was going to bite. I must keep going. I was inches from The Portal. "Hurry!" screamed Sunday. "Faster Ember!" Did he not realise that it was physically impossible for me to go any faster than I already was? One more step. I took it and flung myself through The Portal. I was safe. We were safe.

I stopped and tried to breathe. "Ember! What are you doing? RUN!" Confused, I stumbled on. Why? Why must I run? We were safe, weren't we?

I had assumed the cobra wouldn't be able to come through The Portal, but I was wrong. A deafening, angry hiss told me otherwise. I flew down the thin windowless hallway and crashed through the door at the end. I made the mistake of looking back and found the cobra was only a metre away from me. "HELP!" Sunday yelled as we were dazzled by the illusion of sunlight. "ANYONE, HELP! PLEASE!" Nobody came. We were alone.

I twisted and turned through the maze of pristine streets and skyscrapers, the snake hot on my heels. I felt the ground rumble as it demolished buildings with its colossal tail. Suddenly, there was a sound like thunder and I was blown off my feet.

Chapter 32

"She's alive!"

"Are you sure?"

"Positive. I can feel her pulse."

"Great. Bring her in on a stretcher." Course hands lifted me onto a sheet, and I was hoisted off the ground. "Stay with me, Ember. Stay with me." I wanted so badly to block out the noises that were overwhelming me. I wanted to roll over and fall asleep. "Ember, you must stay awake. Stay with me." There was a ringing in my ears and my chest was tight. What was going on? Where was I? "Everything's going to be just fine." Fine? Fine! Nothing was fine. "Say something to me." I didn't want to talk. I wanted to sleep. "I know you want to go to sleep but you can't. I need you to stay with me, Ember. Open your eyes." I tried to focus and follow the instructions as I was finally placed on a bed.

Tubes pumped stuff into me, and someone squeezed liquids into my ears, eyes and mouth. Then, cold hands massaged soap into my hair and sponged the dirt from my body. I was towelled dry and dressed in clean clothes. I could see and hear but couldn't seem to make sense of anything. Food and water were forced down my throat and then a syringe was jabbed into my arm.

Chapter 33

When I awoke, I was alone. I sat up and looked around. I recognised this room. This was the hospital room I was kept in after I'd jumped from the skyscraper. I swung my legs round and hopped off the bed. There was a glass of water and some kind of yellow cracker on the bedside table. I sipped the water and nibbled the crackers until both were finished. Then I rose and left the room.

The bright ceiling lights in the reception dazzled me. As my eyes were adjusting I saw someone approaching me. I couldn't make out who it was and didn't have time to. As soon as they were within reach of me, they gave me a hard slap in the face. Angry, I shoved them away and stepped back.
"What the-"
"How could you?" It was Alora.
"How could I what?" I asked.
"Don't act the fool, Ember. You know what you did."
"What? I don't get it," I told her.
"Zandar," she answered.
"But I didn't tell anyone he was working for Three. I haven't had the chance! I've been knocked out cold since I got back!" I said, indignantly.
"Well Sunday's been awake, and he's told Storm about this entire fiasco, including Zandar!"

"And how, exactly, is that my fault? And why are you so outraged? Zandar stabbed us all in the back!" I said, my voice rising.

"Back stabber or not, he's been there for me since we were born. And this is your fault because if you'd never have gone to get back Theo, he wouldn't have been discovered, and Neptune would still be alive!" Furious that Alora was pining all of this on me, I turned around and headed back into my hospital room. "Where do you think you're going? You're coming with me. I'm taking you to the Court where you'll be sentenced!"

Chapter 34

Utterly baffled and speechless, I followed Alora out of Peak. She led me down streets that were littered with debris and rubble. I looked around and saw the path of destruction carved by the cobra during its pursuit of us, and the lifeless body of the cobra itself. "What happened? After I got knocked out, I mean," I asked Alora.

"Well, a huge Block was activated, which crippled the snake and threw you off your feet. It also demolished a huge section of the city and killed or injured many of our citizens. After the explosion, about a hundred or so citizens and soldiers rushed out and shot the snake to bits," Alora replied icily. I looked at the cobra and saw thousands of bullet holes all over its scaly body. I nodded and let the information set in.

"Is it safe to be walking around if there are still active Blocks lying about?" I questioned.

"No, but whilst you were away, everyone has been trained to recognise the Blocks. Look, there's one there. You can tell because of the way the surface ripples in the sunlight," she told me. My gaze followed her pointing finger and I see an area on the side of a building that seems to shimmer and flow. "We still haven't figured out how to deactivate them though, just avoid them."

"And were those explosions in the Outside caused by Blocks too?" I asked.

"Yes. Three planted them there to protect their Portal. But it backfired and ended up killing their own creations."

"So, why the heck am I being put on trial?" I finally asked.
"Take a look around, Ember. Do you see the mess you've made? If you'd have just stayed here like you were told to, none of this would have ever happened." Alora replied. I was about to argue when I realised it was true.
"What about Theo? Was I supposed to just leave him there?" I yelled, feeling I had a point to make.
"No, but you going hasn't achieved anything! He's still stuck there, One is in ruins and many of our soldiers and spies are dead." I was hot with rage and stormed off up ahead, without a clue as to where I was going. Alora soon caught up. Wanting to break the awkward silence, I asked; "How about the rest of the army? Did they make it back?"
"Mostly. Some of them were killed after infiltrating Three's Headquarters. Other than that, the mission was as success. We have the captives in Peak," she answered, and gave me a look which told me she was still mad about the whole Zandar thing.
"Alora," I said, "I know Zan was your friend and all, but he did try to kill me, your own brother and a five-year-old. He's totally cruel and a traitor to One."
"I don't want to talk about it, Ember. Besides, we're here."

We entered a large white building. It was grand on the inside. There was a foyer with potted plants and an emerald green carpet. Black and white pictures of old men adorned the walls and white leather sofas were pushed up against the four walls. Alora guided me through a set of double doors and signed something in a notebook. Then she took me into the courtroom. There was another green carpet and eight rows of cushioned seats designated for the jury. At the far end of the room, Storm sat on the bench with the gavel. In front of the bench was a desk and two chairs. Sunday was already sitting at one and I assumed the other was for me. I walked down the aisle between the seated jury members and couldn't help but notice that some of them were familiar. I took my place next to Sunday and the proceedings began. "Ember Jones and Sunday Miller, rise in the face of justice." I stood and felt nerves bubble in my stomach. What were they going to do to me? Lock me up? Execute me? I thought that seemed a little extreme but nothing seemed too over the top for the people down here. Me and Sunday exchanged a nervous glance as Storm continued. "You both have been summoned here today for your sentencing. You both are charged with the utter destruction of our city. If neither of you had gone to save Theo, those snake mutations wouldn't have been unleashed upon One. In addition, you are charged with the death of Neptune Wilson, who was killed by a Block planted by Three, Maynard Williams, who was blown to pieces after you shoved him into a Block and Betta Brown who also died trying to save your life. You may be seated. If anyone has anything to add speak now or forever hold your peace."

"That's ridiculous!" I shouted, outraged. "I didn't ask them to come and save me! Neptune swam ahead and got blown up and Betta's face melted! The only death that was actually my fault was Maynard's!" Nobody seemed to care.

The sentencing lasted about three hours. People like Aster and Pluto tried to defend us but others including Zale and Alora wanted us punished. I could see the hurt in Sunday's eyes when Alora, his own sister, betrayed him. After discussing a suitable punishment for half hour, Storm banged his gavel down on the wooden surface of the bench. "Ember The Fire Starter-" Storm began.

"What?" I yelled, jumping from my seat, "Is that my name now? I'll give you Fire Starter! What fire?" I asked.

"It's a metaphor, Ember. Now silence. Ember The Fire Starter and Sunday Miller, I sentence you both to ten years of exile."
"WHAT?" Sunday also jumped up from his seat. "We don't deserve this! None of this is our fault!" We were both lifted off of our feet by uniformed men. Me and Sunday shouted insults at Storm, Alora, and Zale as we were marched out of the courtroom and back through the foyer. The entire jury and Storm followed behind the men carrying us. I was confused and sad that we had been exiled. This place wasn't my home. But it was Sunday's. And if we were exiled, how would I get Theo back?

We were marched to the very edge of One and dumped on the dusty ground. I stood up and brushed the dust from my clothes. Directly in front of me was the crumbling concrete skyscraper that Sunday and I had climbed up all those months ago. "You can't do this!" I shouted, "It isn't fair!" But nobody cared. Nobody was even listening. The uniformed men picked up their shotguns and began closing in on me and Sunday. We backed away. I felt an odd tingling sensation running down my back as I was pushed into the Dome. The last thing I saw before I was plunged into darkness was Alora's smirking face.

Chapter 35

My head slammed against the ground as I fell back through the Dome. I felt Sunday drag me up and wrap me in his arms.
"No going back," he sighed.
"Not even through The Portal?" I asked.
"No. But even if we could get in, we'd only be kicked out again." We slumped on the floor and sat together, keeping each other warm. Storm's words rolled around in my head. Ember The Fire Starter. I guessed that's how people would remember me.
"Hey," I said, breaking the heavy silence, "I've made a start on that prophecy. I've destroyed part of One. No saving yet, however."
"I guess you're right, Miss Fire Starter," Sunday replied.
"Don't."
"At least you got a cool name. I'm just plain old Sunday Miller."
"Jealous, I see!" We both laughed. Anything to lighten the mood.

In the end we both slept. Restlessly, but still, it was a few hours of rest. My dreams were filled with snakes and water and fire. My heart was pounding when I awoke, and I was baking hot. I sat bolt upright and took deep breaths.

I couldn't believe what had happened over the last few months. My world had become a living nightmare and it all began when Dad left. First we had to move into a crummy flat, and it was just outside there that me and Theo had fallen down into an Underground world on the brink of war and learnt that I was the key to some stupid old prediction. Then we were torn apart from each other, and I nearly fell to my death. I had gotten so close to saving him only to get ripped away from him again. Then I had been chased by bloodthirsty, million-foot-long snakes and finally sentenced to exile!

Sunday stirred in his sleep. He looked so peaceful. It was at that moment that I realised I truly loved him. How could I not. He'd saved my life so many times, risked everything for Theo and me, and hadn't complained once that I had gotten him banished from his home. Planting a kiss on his forehead, I laid down close beside him and stared up into the dark abyss.

There was a huge gaping hole in my heart where Theo should've been, mum should've been, my sisters should've been. I held onto the hope that Theo was still alive, useful to Three in some way. Rescuing my brother and getting us home was my only priority now. Maybe Sunday could come with us seeing as he'd been exiled from his home, I thought. If only we weren't so alone. Then I suddenly realised we weren't. Hadn't Sunday said there were hundreds of Defts out here, exiled from One just like us? Maybe we could find them and their city, if it existed. Maybe they would help us?

A wave of exhaustion washed over me, and my eyelids felt overwhelmingly heavy. I closed my eyes, wanting to escape reality for a little longer. The last thoughts I had before I drifted off to sleep were; Storm was right about one thing. I am no longer plain old Ember Jones.

I am The Fire Starter.

END OF BOOK ONE

About the Author

Jessica is just 11 years old, a secondary school student who lives with her mum, dad, and little sister in Southampton. She loves cats, the colour green, tidiness, dark chocolate and chicken Kiev's (not on the same plate!). However, her biggest passion is storytelling, and she can usually be found with her nose in a book. She is already chasing her dream of becoming a world-renowned author, and if you've made it this far, you don't need telling that it is only a matter of time. This, her debut novel, will be the first instalment in a trilogy of books and the proceeds will go to The MS Society, a charity that has recently become important to Jessica and her family.
They could not be prouder of her.

Printed in Great Britain
by Amazon

25951097R00071